The Snowman of Nalanda

Roshan

Leadstart
INKSTATE

ISBN 978-93-90040-35-3
Copyright © Roshan, 2020

First published in India 2021 by Leadstart Inkstate
A Division of One Point Six Technologies Pvt Ltd

Sales Office:
Unit No.25/26, Building No.A/1,
Near Wadala RTO,
Wadala (East), Mumbai – 400037 India
Phone: +91 969933000
Email: info@leadstartcorp.com
www.leadstartcorp.com

Disclaimer: The views expressed in this book are those of the Author and do not pertain to be held by the Publisher.

Editor: Kavya Shree
Cover: Ashwini Jadhav
Layouts: Kshitij Dhawale

Dedicated to Love

About the Author

Roshan lives in Jharkhand. He has done his schooling from Sainik School, Nalanda, and graduation from Tata Institute of Social Sciences (TISS), Hyderabad. He is also a poet, has written a book named 100 Titleless poems. This is his first novel. He loves travelling to distant places on his motorcycle.

Acknowledgements

The yeti has always remained in my imaginations. There have been several expeditions in the 1950's to unfold the mystery but it has remained concealed. It attracted my attention and I decided to write a book on it. My flight of fancy opened the door to a secret world. I am not the only one puzzled by the yeti — there have many explorers before who tried to explore the secret. These explorers have been my inspiration to peep into the myth. I added the manure of my fantasy into the garden of mind which blossomed into a story, and I want to share it with the world.

I have been extremely thankful to Balram, Prabhutosh and Joshi for their support in my journey. I am most thankful to my father who pushed me to learn the art of crafting stories using the secret ingredient of patience, which I still lack in plenty. The book is the result of my obsession with the yeti. I want to believe in the myth. Furthermore, I am grateful to Himanshu for adding his critical view towards the book.

I would like to thank my brother and sister for their immense patience with my raw story and providing with me with their love and support. At last, I am thankful to Dr Suja Kurian and Dr Niji Rachel Varughese for their medical assistance.

Contents

1

The Hunter and the Monk

The Nalanda monastery was a dream place to explore the barren territory of life. It was among one of the greatest centre of learning in the medieval times. There were ten thousand students residing in the monastery studying different subjects. Bidyasagar was the most respected master of the monastery. Once he was a merciless hunter and a dacoit in the area but nobody knows this fact regarding him. Killing was fun for him.

Once during his olden days, when he was walking back after killing a deer, he met a Buddhist monk. There were rumours that rich merchants are taking on fake attire of monks to pass his territory. He was told by his spy a rich merchant will be passing his territory dressed as one. He was well prepared. He sharpened his long knife and took it with him. He was extremely happy; he was going to loot a hefty sum from the passing merchant.

In the morning he was waiting eagerly for the merchant in the deep forest. He was patient. Since morning not a single person had passed this place. Time was passing but no one had come. He was told by his spy that the merchant would pass early in the morning. It was already 10. He was walking, restless, all around the forest, thinking the merchant would not come. As soon as he decided to leave, he heard the sound of footsteps. He hid in the canopy of bushes. There was a monk coming towards him. He was alert; he was sure he would be the same merchant who was trying to fool him. He jumped out of the bush and took out the sharp knife he always carried with him.

The monk seemed fearless, unmoved by his sudden appearance. Bidyasagar said in a thunderous voice, "Hand me this bag of yours and I will let you go." The monk peacefully said, "I cannot give this bag to you." Bidyasagar asked again but he refused to give him the bag at any cost.

Bidyasagar was getting angry. He threatened to kill him but the monk seemed determined. He said calmly, "Gold coins would take you nowhere, instead will keep you chained." He spoke to him as if he was a friend. Hearing the mention of gold coins, he became greedier. He was sure the bag had coins of gold. He wanted the bag to be in his possession. The monk said, "Save yourself from the demon within, I can help you out. I can see you are untouched by the gift of kindness." Bidyasagar was getting desperate and he wanted to take the bag from the monk's hand. The greed took over him. He took out his knife, stabbed the monk and took away the little bag from the bleeding man. Hours later, the monk died alone in the forest. Bidyasagar brought the bag to his house and opened it expecting gold coins but found books and pages of verses. He was frustrated at the sight, unable to understand why someone will give away his life for these useless verses and books. He again ran towards the forest thinking the merchant might be on the way. He reached the same spot and found the monk dead. He buried him in the forest and began waiting for the merchant. No one came.

He walked back home, irritated with the false message

from his spy. He kept those pages of verses and texts in one corner. He walked out and returned late in the night. He was getting bored and wasn't in a good mood. He could not understand how the monk knew he had come for the gold coins. He realized the greed was evident in his eyes. Finally, he decided to have a look at those books in the bag for which the monk gave away his life. He first came across a page where a poem was written. He began reading it.

Siddhartha

Death was unknown to him,

So was life.

He was dancing on the lotuses,

Grasses were unknown to him.

There was an artificial covering,

In which he was wrapped in,

He left his beloved queen

And his son,

As he left the gates of palace,

He encountered a demon,

Speaking verses of malice.

He wanted to end the cycle of suffering

And know the reality as it is,

Instead of the world, he wanted to seize

The inner world with compassion and peace.

He practiced every extreme

And tried to get rid of

The hellish organism in him,

Which was making the truth dim,

But after years of practicing the extremes

He has to quit.

Then he decided to walk the middle way,

He begins to reach closer to the truth

Day by day.

He begins to get lost in himself,

He had tried all the help

But one has to walk his own way.

He learnt to play

With his breaths.

For days he remained in meditation

Like some meditating cat.

He could see what made life miserable

And what was the bait?

It was the bird of desire,

The demon appeared again

But he knew he was a liar.

He liked something about the poem—the man in it. Bidyasagar could feel it is nothing but the desires which had kept him trapped in the illusionary house. This was his life; he was locked in a house without windows where nothing could enter—not the sunlight, not the moonlight, not even a firefly. It was a house with close walls. He was aware of the fact that whoever Siddhartha was, he too was puzzled by the mystery of life. He needed an idea to initiate the chain reaction in his mind. The atom of life is empty like our hearts. He has witnessed that demon himself. He wanted to get rid of the demon but he was unable to do so. He was relieved to know that someone had beaten the demon before. His name was Siddhartha. He wanted to beat his demons like the man in the poem.

He had never heard of Siddhartha before but every book the monk had was dedicated to him. He liked the poem; he got interested in the books. There were few other books on medicinal herbs and plants as well. For the next few days he did nothing but read one book after another. He got lost in the sea of words. These were the books which the monk was carrying to the Nalanda monastery. It was from a note inside he found that out. He thought of visiting the place. There were many more books left to read, he figured he would read them on his way to Nalanda. He had been living here in the forest for a long time. There was a map along with the texts. He was sure it would take him to the monastery where this monk had been heading. He understood the monk was a poet and an Ayurveda teacher. There were few more pages of verses written by the dead monk. Apart from it, there were many more poems which he must read. He began reading another one by the monk.

A River of Fireflies

A river of fireflies was flowing through the dark forest.

It appeared darkness was their nest.

I was passing by like a stranger to the wild.

A thought came like a breeze and I smiled

It told me oh passing traveler,

Life is nothing but a river.

Why you remain always in hurry.

Everyone is part of that simple story.

Life then death,

After it has attained its full length and breadth.

Live a little more,

Go little far off to that distant shore.

Become that jolly grasshopper.

Don't let those little dreams to get hamper

In the temporary flood of emotional turmoil.

Add little manure of happiness in the inner soil.

Grow plant of hope from the seeds of despair.

Become that curious fox and that dancing hare.

He understood what the monk was trying to convey through the poem. Life is a short affair. It would pass away like a river. He was explaining some of the simple rules to live this life of ours to the fullest. We should live freely, without any boundaries in our mind. There should not be despair but hope in our eyes as hope is the most powerful tool life has invented in its evolution. He began rethinking his life as a hunter; it was a cruel pursuit. A hunter must be cruel. A hunter cannot be kind, but it was kindness he needed to learn in life. Kindness was suddenly a virtue, a virtue which he lost with time while following his cruel pursuit. He realized killing the monk was not a mistake but a choice which he made out of greed. The more he thought of the monk, the more he hated himself. There was no one in his life who could have made him learn kindness before. He realized that kindness is contagious. He was raised with cruelty. He never knew what kindness is until he met the monk. The monk was kind even when he came to loot him. The only good thing he did in the past: he learnt to read and write. He wanted to save him from dying now but the monk was already dead. He made a little temple at his grave out of great respect for him. He was puzzled by his thoughts. He had understood he had made a grave mistake by killing the monk.

But he was excited to know more about Siddhartha and left for Nalanda. In the morning when he began walking, the weather was pleasant but it didn't stay so for long. It began to rain heavily, a storm unleashed from the sky. Every time he closed his eyes, the monk appeared in his memory mirror. He wanted to get away from that memory but one cannot run from his ghost. We all have ghosts of past chasing our present life. Among the books, he began reading the ones on Ayurveda.

After a while he entered the deep, dark forest where he felt a little peaceful. He could see a herd of wild deer passing by. He had never found the forest so peaceful but reading the dead monk's writing and the books he was carrying to Nalanda gave him a sense of peace which he didn't think existed in this world. He was a changed man; deer was nothing but food for him in the past but today he could see the beauty in the way they were crossing the jungle. There was grace in their running. He never felt that way in the past but was looking at them like never before. He sat under a tree and began reading another poem by the dead monk. Every time he read his poems he is filled with guilt but even then he could not resist his writings. There were many more books in the bag which he had not read, all dedicated to Siddhartha. He has begun to like Siddhartha even without knowing much about him. There was a mystery about this man who needed to be demystified. He wanted to know more and more about him. He read another poem written between the little pages.

Little crab dreams wrapped in hard shell,

Walks the desolate shores of life

Looking for shelter, which can be only our heart.

That's the best place for a dream.

Little tadpole dreams swim across the dark rivers,

Dreaming of turning into a magical frog

And jump through the craters of moon

And marshes of mars.

Little fish dreams dances across the ocean,

Dreaming of turning into that whale

Whose fin cut routes across the glaciers

And the sea.

My dream is to get rid of

The hellish organism in me.

I must be free.

Everybody should dream of turning into Siddhartha

And attain peace for eternity.

He liked it. Every time he read his poems, the words of the dead monk revealed something to him. He understood the monk was talking about the importance of dreams. Dreams have the power to transform the inner landscape of mind. He realized it was the monk's dream to achieve that serenity in life, a serenity which Siddhartha attained. After reading he began looking at the silent sky. Far off on a branch, a yellow bird was chirping a song. The deer were gone but soon came squirrels, running one behind another. It was a beautiful sight. Something melted inside his heart and he was sobbing moments later, filled with remorse. He should not have killed that kind monk but that is done now. He began cursing himself again for the act of the murder. The more he read his words, the more he felt at peace with himself. He has killed hundreds of animals and all their faces were running in his head like a river of shadows. He has never cried before. The first tear which fell from his eyes, fell on the ground and turned into a white flower. He could feel lotuses blooming in the pond of his heart.

We all suffer secretly. He never thought he would cry in grief for someone. Life is a completely alien creature for humans. Things go unexpected here. He looked more into the bag of books he was carrying. There were several other books on Ayurveda left to read. There were even picture of leaves. He was interested in the medicinal plants because he needed them when he got wounded in fights with wild animals. There were hundreds of wounds on his body, all signs of his brutality.

Close to the forest where he lived, there was a village where every year a fight championship was arranged. Nobody has ever defeated him in a fight. Every year he won the bloody battles. He survived those wounds because of his little knowledge of the medicinal plants in the forest.

He was thrilled to know about Siddhartha, to read the poems of the dead monk and explore the medicinal world more. There was never a thirst inside him to know the world but now he wanted to know everything about it.

He stood up and began walking again like a prince. He decided to stay in jungle for few days having developed a liking for silence. The next day, he came across a lake, it was beautiful. He sat there looking at the little waves hitting the shore. There were birds flying far off in the sky. The sun was rising from the cocoon of darkness. He could see the moon turning into the sun. He could see the sun turning into a butterfly and leaving the shore of darkness. His shores of imagination began to expand. There were many questions bubbling in his little mind. The sun rose like a child and its yellow fingers began playing with the wind. He could see the reflection of the sun in the sparkling water. He began to think everything is nothing but a shadow, even this body of bones. It will pass, this moment.

He could even see the shadow of the flying birds in the water; he could see the shadow of the sun. He concluded nothing is real in this world, not even the sun. His belief got stronger that everything is a shadow but a shadow of what?

He began thinking but he had no answer. He walked to a tree, plucked few fruits and began eating. He has been a hunter all his life but he didn't feel the need to kill these creatures anymore. Something strange was happening within him in the forest. He could feel a spirit around, doing something to his heart. His thoughts were changing like the weather. Sometimes his mind got cloudy; sometimes the sun began to shine in his inner sky. The world suddenly began to look mysterious to him. Everything was strange, this life, this jungle.

In the afternoon, he found the shade of a tree. Sometimes in life all you want is to sit under a tree silently. It's worth it, the silence, and the leafy ambience around. He lay there for an afternoon nap. He got a very peaceful sleep that afternoon. When he woke up, it was evening. He was happy. Everything looked pleasant to his eyes. At night the forest became cruel, there were sounds of different creatures coming from the heart of the dark forest. Suddenly he felt two bright eyes approaching him. It was a tiger. Its body was shining in the bright moonlight. He could hear the breaths of the tiger. Bidyasagar felt his life will be over in moments even though he has faced them in wild before but with weapons. Death was certain, he realized, but to his surprise the tiger came and stood just before him, looking him into his eyes. And then it left quietly.

He could not make any thing out of it. Why the tiger would not attack him? He began thinking but he could not get any answer. *Maybe I have longer to live but why god would spare me? I am a murderer.* He felt how one feels when death is too close but he remembered there was no such fear in the eyes of the dying monk. He died as if death meant nothing to him.

In the morning, he left the forest and began walking towards Nalanda monastery. After walking for nine days he reached the monastery. He could see the grandness of it. It looked beautiful from outside. There were two gates to walk inside the monastery but there were guards at each of them. These were not ordinary guards but learned men who were appointed at the gate for conducting tests of the visitors. Not everyone who comes here got a chance to read in the grandest monastery of the world. He walked towards the gate and as expected, the guard stopped him and said, "You cannot walk inside until you pass the test."

Bidyasagar replied, "What kind of test?"

"It's a simple test. First you have to tell me the reason for your visit. On that ground, I will ask further questions."

He said, "I am a poet and an Ayurveda teacher. You can see I have a bag full of books on medicine and poems."

The guard said, "You have to tell me a poem and it must be composed at this very moment, on life." Further, he was asked for the cure of jaundice. Bidyasagar hesitated as he was not a poet but a hunter. He could not come up with anything, neither for the poem nor for the cure. He failed the test. He was asked to come again later. Bidyasagar decided he would become the greatest poet ever born on the planet. *I would return one day to these gates and I would be welcomed.* He left the place with a will to learn the art of poetry and medicine. He knew no way to turn into a poet. There was no way but the way itself.

He was disheartened by it. He was so close to the monastery. He could see its grandness from there. He wanted very badly to walk inside. It was the greatest building he had ever laid his eyes on, spread across thousands of acres. He could hear the chanting of prayers. He could see the top of a multistorey building in the middle of the monastery. There was another world behind these walls but he couldn't walk inside. He was sad and quiet on the way back. It was the first time he realized how rejection feels but he was determined to set foot inside the monastery. But at present, he had no idea where to go. This was a new place for him. He went and sat in the bazaar, amidst the great crowd. There were all sorts of things in the bazaar—potters were selling various forms of pots, some were selling honey, others clay tablets. He had a desire to eat a sweet which was being prepared at some distance from him. He reached the sweet shop and asked for what he wanted. The sweet was tastier than expected. There he heard two people talking about the Kingdom of Vishaka. Immediately, he decided to visit the kingdom. He asked the sweet-shop owner where the kingdom was located and its directions. The shopkeeper told him it would take three days to reach there. He decided he would come back to Nalanda after he had learnt more about both subjects. Till then he would roam here and there. He first decided to visit Vishaka and left for it alone and disheartened.

He came across a small village where he decided to rest for the night. He knocked on the gate of a house there and an old lady came out. She asked him who he was.

Bidyasagar said he was a wanderer and he needed a place to stay for the night. The lady allowed him and gave him some food too. He asked the old lady if she lived by herself. The old lady replied, "I live with my husband."

"And children?" He was curious.

"I had two sons, both died in the war with Seina. The war took place few years back between the kingdoms of Vishaka and Seina. The king of Seina had become over ambitious and decided to raid the territory of Vishaka. Vishaka despite being a small kingdom retaliated with courage. The war lasted for two months; Vishaka kept fighting the war with its small army. Vishaka lost the war after fighting a courageous battle and the prince was killed too. This left the king depressed. It is said the death of his son created a void in his heart. He was never seen laughing again."

Bidyasagar liked the compassionate old lady. She was living in very miserable conditions. During nights she would wake up sobbing. She had a pet cat who was her companion. He never saw her husband speak. Bidyasagar could see what a war could do to people. It could make a man lonely. She still prepared chapattis for her sons but gave them to her calf instead. These creatures were her companion in her loneliness. The cat sat on the wall and mewed.

The cat had befriended a bat who tells the cat secrets of the jungle in an unknown language.

This jungle of chaos had a hyena and her children who once fell in the well of darkness. It started raining and the water in the well began to rise. The hyena first tried to save her children, by putting them above the surface of rising water. She tried very hard but when death approached near, she used her children as bricks to keep herself above the water by standing on their bodies. Her children died and she survived. Another tale was of a leopard who murdered his own cubs for nothing. These tales depressed the cat. *This world is cruel and I can't deal with it.*

The bat then said to the cat, "Yes, the world is cruel but there are stories of sparrows who gave away their lives to save their chicks from the attack of wild vultures. There was a dog who gave away his life to save his master from a poisonous cobra. The bat said the world is binary, the good and the evil exist together.

Bidyasagar had a strange gift—he could understand the languages of the creatures. He was listening carefully to the *secret* conversation between the cat and the bat. He agreed with the bat but he also had an accompanying thought—the world is cruel because we have made it so. We ourselves have created the net of cruelty around. He felt embarrassed because for long he has been an active element in turning the world cruel. He agreed with the bat that cruelty lies within. Bidyasagar kept hearing the words of the bat. He was making sense. Moments later he got up and sat beside the old lady. The hand pump in the middle of the verandah was rusted. He could see its shadow in the light of the lantern. Suddenly, he realized he had his answer. He knows everything is shadow of time. Everything around us is a shadow of time, even the human civilization. Shadow is not a reality but a fallacy. Next day he decided to leave for the Kingdom of Vishaka which was far away as there was a strange craving to visit the place. He wanted to meet the king, a worthy ruler who lost his son for his kingdom. The king should be praised for his bravery.

He would never forget the kind hospitality of that old lady who treated him like her own son. He learnt a lot in the way. The closer he came to the kingdom of Vishaka, the more his excitement grew. His mind began speculating his future.

2

Kingdom of Vishaka

He woke up in the morning and asked for permission to leave the house of the old lady. He began to walk through the grasses towards Vishaka. He was excited to reach the glorious kingdom. His mind was getting heavy with the thoughts of past. The past always remains standing in the horizon of thoughts. He could see the ghosts walking around wearing the masks of different sorts. The twinkling stars in the sky of past still radiates beautiful light from its core. Everything decays, even past, but its imprint on the present lasts forever. He could change all that he was in the past and he could master his present. He began to believe he could change his little destiny. Once he reached Vishaka, he heard an announcement from the king. There were drumbeats signifying the announcement regarding the marriage of the princess. There was a wild game of hunting organized by the king. The victor would be married to the princess. It was an archery competition where a man-eating tiger was to be killed. For years he had practiced archery to hunt. He didn't know why but he wanted to participate in the competition. There was no reason for it; he had no desire to marry the princess but simply an urge born out of his barren heart, an urge to see the great king and know him personally.

He reached the spot where the ceremony was organized. There was a mandap of flowers in the centre and horses were running around. It was here he saw the princess for the first time. She was beautiful. And now he wanted to win, her beauty pushing him. They had to hunt down a wild tiger which had killed almost dozens of people.

It was not an ordinary tiger. For a month, the best hunters in the kingdom tried to hunt it down but it was a very shrewd creature. Hence, the king decided to use the opportunity to seek arrangement for marriage of her only daughter as kings have respect for brave men.

The rules are simple: the tiger must be hunted down in a day. There were princes from nearby kingdoms and many noble men who were participating in the game. There were hundreds of contenders. The tiger could be anywhere in the jungle. Soon came the news the tiger has killed one prince. It created panic amongst the other contenders but not in the heart of Bidyasagar. He was determined to kill the tiger; he had done it before. Morning passed, afternoon arrived but he could not spot the animal. News of deaths kept coming. It was in the evening when he found the tiger. It attacked him from nowhere. He fought with his sword and soon the tiger vanished. He had his eyes in every direction but he knew tigers have a habit to attack from behind. He decided to make a mask from wood and put it on backwards. This was a trick to confuse the tiger which has always worked in the past. The tiger attacked him from front, confused by the two faces. Bidyasagar got his chance. He fired his arrow, his aim meticulous. It hit the tiger in the eyes. It went blind. Soon the writing of that monk began appearing in his mind. He did not want to kill the tiger. He could feel now the pain the beast was in. He decided not to use any more arrows. He didn't want to kill it but the animal perished to its wounds few minutes later.

The king announced the marriage and he was married to the princess in the mandap of flowers. Few days passed and he forgot about the tiger. He was in love with the princess. Soon, even the princess fell in love with Bidyasagar. A month passed. Bidyasagar forgot everything, including the killing of the monk. He was the King of the Vishaka now. The old king had abandoned his throne as there was no heir and passed it to Bidyasagar. There was news from the royal spies. The kingdom of Seine was again preparing for another war with Vishaka. Bidyasagar did not want a war but he had to protect his people. He knew what a war can do, he remembered the old lady. He tried every means to avoid it. His ministers began doubting his courage. People thought he wanted to evade war by all means. They thought him to be a coward.

He, though, tried harder to evade it. He even offered all the treasure from the royal treasury. The King of Seina also thought him to be a coward. The next morning the news reached that the kingdom of Seine was going to attack tomorrow. There was no plan ready yet. The war was certain now. Bidyasagar had failed to evade it. He had little choice now.

He began planning. He called his commander in chief and asked how many horses they had. The commander in chief gave him the exact number: 5000. Bidyasagar began to think. The tiger hunt had taught him that masks can bring victory. He needed a mask where he could hide his 5000 horsemen. The war began. The enemies were four times the size of his army. Defeat appeared certain.

He must make a plan where he could hide his 5000 horsemen. Finally, he was able to come up with an idea. He read all the medicinal books which belonged to the monk in the due course of war. He sent few of his men to bring selected medicinal herbs from the forest. The war began, hundreds of soldiers died on both side. He could see with his eyes the futility of the war. Every day hundreds of soldiers were dying. He felt the pain for even the opposite army. He mourned the loss of every soldier in the battlefield.

The herbs his men were in search for were to be used to save as many lives as possible. The war continued for a month and it appeared Vishaka would lose the battle. But on the 31st day, the horsemen suddenly attacked when there was a dry storm. There was zero visibility but they remained unfazed, trained for hardships. This helped; they were equipped for the storm. The hidden horsemen ended the war in few hours. Vishaka had won but thousands had died. Another news came soon after—the princess had died a week ago. This was not conveyed to Bidyasagar as it could have affected the due course of war.

This left him bewildered. He could not believe his ears. It appeared everything had come to an end. He loved his wife. He cried and cried. He asked god why he had done this to him. It was the first time he had fallen in love with somebody. He cursed the gods but suddenly his past memories filled him. All the animals he had killed, the monk, he could feel their pain. He understood why god was causing him such a suffering. He told himself he deserved all the suffering.

Next morning, he abandoned the throne and walked away, into the forest. For days, he mourned the loss of the princess. He would walk aimlessly, from morning to night. He would walk any path which came his way. He was a pathless wanderer now. He was looking for peace but there was only suffering and pain.

One night he was lying down on the grass. The sky was clear. He could see thousands of stars twinkling. He could feel the nature of life is suffering. Nobody can escape it, not even a king. He has begun to see the face of shadow. He was right, everything in this world is shadow of time. Everything is destructible, every inch of life and dreams. He could feel the futility of chasing anything. Time destroys everything, even this world will get destroyed one day. The way he lost his beloved princess made him feel powerless in front of that chaotic force which runs the world. He could feel the sorrow of all the people who lost their loved ones in the war. He began cursing himself again for the killings he did under the influence of his evil self as a hunter. He had killed many animals as a hunter and far more men as a king during the war. Although, as a king he tried to save the lives of as many as he could through the medicinal herbs.

Today he was thinking again of the monk. His knowledge of medicine and Ayurveda helped save hundreds of lives but he killed that monk. He cried in remorse but this is the tragedy of life; one cannot undo a past act. He felt miserable. It was a sin which will follow him till hell, or even after, who knows. He wanted to run to that moment and wished he could have read his poems and the books before. He would have let the monk go; the monk would have passed the test at Nalanda. He thought about the many more poems the monk would have written. He murdered not just the monk but his poetry too. He wanted to write like the monk. He had taken the life of a person who could have been his teacher, the greatest sin one could do. The monk is teaching him even after his death through his writings. This is the beauty of great people; they teach us even after they are gone.

He wanted to touch the dead monk's feet. Soon he was lost in the memory of his beloved princess. She has taught him the art to love. For the first time a desire rose from his heart to write something. He was sailing at the moment in a sea of emotions. He wrote his first poem sitting under the stars in her memory.

The phosphorescent lights dissolve in my heart

Has hundreds of sun in it,

You sip inside my earth

Like the raindrops

And get collected in my little cracks.

Time will refine you like some wine

And my lips will always be dying to evaporate time

Like swans evaporate from the wet surface of lake,

Suddenly without a noise.

I will do it just by blowing a gasp of my melodious breath

In your ears,

The sweet fragrance of innocence

Will make this wild bee dance,

Someday like some drunkard.

I have seen my bulbul getting very close to turn into maqbool,

But the child in you

Never let it happen,

The transformation and you remain left in you

Like silence remains left in the surrounding after
thunder.

You are a city

Which I always want to win

But when my heart reaches close to victory,

I simply return

Without a pinch of gold in my hand,

You may call me a beggar even if I am a king,

Oh, that madness, that feeling

Of touching your shadow

Fills my barren craters with grasshoppers.

And they sing like never before.

The warmth in you

Make great migration of wild cranes

From their cold islands

Towards your warm shore.

I wish only I could love you more

And more and more.

Sometimes I feel when scorpions in me

Hide back beneath the bottom of stones,

I am here just for your love,

I have no other work unlike all men,

How a peacock could not love the rain,

Even if the drops are poured

From a great distance,

At whose heart, no peacock will ever reach,

Something in me always gets torn apart,

Which only you can stitch,

Sometimes I feel you are a tailor bird

When I see the perfection of yours

In the art of stitching a man's heart

And you do it with great ease,

Show me your wings,

Oh tailor bird,

I want to see them,

Kiss them with a love

Which can make your nerve go impatient.

Sometimes I become some sailor in some cursed ship,

And you, my hope

To land on some port.

When my all allies fail,

I always look towards you for friendship and support,

My queen even though

I have lost my kingdom,

Please don't go.

Stay, I will give you my love

As a dove gives it her lady dove.

We will hang in the branches of *rajnigandha*

Looking at the moon,

I will become a desert only to gift you a sand dune.

He felt very happy post writing. There were tears in his eyes for the dead monk whose spirit has taught him the art to write, but he needed to master it. He wanted to master the art of writing like the monk; he would remain his teacher even after his death. He felt real joy, joy which he not felt even after winning the war. He understood why the monk wrote—it frees you from the clutches of empire of time. The emperor of the empire of time is cruel; it gives you a star one moment and the next takes away the moon. He never let the stars twinkle for long in your barren sky. With the going of the moon from his life, his nights were darker than ever. Lost in thoughts he slept. That night he saw a beautiful dream. He was walking again with the princess in a garden of roses beside the pond of white lotuses. She was laughing. The sun was rising like a mysterious tree from the seed of darkness. Birds were flying in the blue sky. A golden feather was falling from the sky, slowly like snow. Both were buzzing in the garden like bees. A peacock was dancing unfurling its grand wings. He wanted to live thousand years in that moment with her. They started running and turned into a deer. They had a strange smile on their faces. Suddenly, he woke up and realized it was a dream. Tears began falling from his eyes. He thought if he hadn't killed the monk, the fate would not have cursed him in such a way.

He imagined his life if his wife were still alive. His life had become a tale of three loves—poetry, princess and his interest to explore the medicinal world of Ayurveda. *If they would have told me she was sick, I could have saved her.* For them war was more important than her life but for him love was more important than war.

He won the war but lost her. This thought turned him sick. The medicines written in the book of monk could have saved her. He decided he would not let anybody lose their loved ones. He would save life while once upon a time he used to take it.

Till now he has just wandered in the jungle looking for animals. He has killed tigers, elephants, rhinos and leopards. Now he wanted to conserve life, life even in its minute form. He gave away eating of flesh of any kind. He has been killing animals since childhood. He suddenly realized how cruel it was. He waited there on the little pond. In summer everything got dry, the water hole became the best place to wait for the animals. He has mastered the art of hunting. Everyone cannot be a hunter but every hunter knows the value of kindness more than anybody because they have been cruel for too long. Cruelty should be left behind in life. Compassion should be praised. He now knew more than cruelty compassion was a virtue which every man required to live a happy life.

He decided to walk to the bazaar. He loved to sit silently there and observe people. He sat in a shop and began looking at the world around. He saw a bird catcher selling hundreds of birds. He bought all the birds and freed them. He saw them leaving the cage. He also prayed to god to free him from his cage. Life has turned into a cage of memories. Those memories are so painful, remembering them brings tears into his eyes. There was change in the behavior of birds once they were released in the free air. The birds are meant to wander the sky. Cages make them sick; it kills their heart. Cages are nothing but walls of iron which encloses the freedom of the soul. The soul is meant to be free. He still has many coins left with him. He began to think he could free thousands of birds from cages of all kinds. Once he used to cage a golden bird in his hut when he lived the life of a hunter. Once he loved the sight of a caged bird but he was not same person now. He had killed birds with his arrow; he used birds to improve his aim. He could feel he needed something more to learn to become a great poet. He was missing something. He has learned a lot in the past but there remained something else to learn. He is in pursuit of knowing something more mysterious.

After roaming a while in the bazaar, he goes to the river for bathing. He has always loved rivers. He swam, imagining himself to be a wild crane which has lost its partner. He has observed cranes never change their partners. He began to think what keeps a crane tied to the other crane. It has to be love. He also wished to spend his life with a *crane* that was now dead. He dived deep inside the heart of the river. He saw a group of wild fishes swimming towards him. He could hear the conversation of those schools of fishes. One black fish was talking about how much he loved the moon. That fish thought it eats away the moon in a month. It considered the moon a flower which disappeared every month. They always wondered why only single moon grew every month. Why there can't be thousands of moons. There could be thousands of fishes from a single fish then why there could not be a forest of moons. This was the dream of that fish, to swim in the forest of moons. Every night he witnessed the forest of stars. The fish swam in the reflection of those stars.

Soon he heard the voice of a blue fish which was complaining to the black fish. It said, "There is a hidden shark in the river." The black fish replied, "Sharks do not exist in rivers. It is a creature of the sea." The blue fish said, "This is a myth. It's a mysterious creature and it is behind the missing fishes. Every day some fishes are missing in the river. I have no evidence but I will prove it." Bidyasagar was horrified that there was a shark in the mighty river. He could feel the blue fish was telling the truth. He could also sense the lurking danger around. He decided to save the school of fishes from the shark. He made a little tent close to the bank of the river and settled in. Few days passed, he could not find the shark but the fishes continued to go missing. The decreasing fish population was worrying the head of the little fish community. Fishes began to believe in the shark theory. Fear was dissolved in every inch of water. No fish was safe.

Bidyasagar brought a dead fish that had died minutes ago to use it as bait. He cuts the fish, letting the blood flow into the water.

Like each time before, his trick worked. The *wolf fish* came out of the shadows and into the light. It was a really big fish but not a shark. He had made a poisoned arrow but he had also taken a vow not to kill any creature again. But he acted upon his instincts, killing the fish. The smaller fishes were saved. They will never know this has been done by Bidyasagar. He was sad he broke his vow of not killing any creature. He sat and thought for a day. What he did was right or wrong? Should he have passed without interfering in the fishy discourse? He should have not gotten involved in the matter but it would have been wrong to leave them at the mercy of the god. He vowed he will never use violence in his life apart from such times when somebody's life is in danger because of some evil force. He promised to god he would not kill a kind soul. He was sure he would not need to use violence again. He would turn into a monk when he grows old, he promised to himself.

He walked to the bazaar again to pass the day. He had been looking to go somewhere but he couldn't decide. There must be a quiet place where he could spend a year. He has been in the forest most of his life. He wanted to explore a new territory. He sat in the same shop in which he used to sit and drink mahuaa. After drinking the fermented drink, he began to think where to go. He was listening intently the conversations going on nearby. He liked listening to people. There was a man from the mountains. He was a sherpa. He had come here for buying spices. He was telling a group of people about a Yeti–the snowman. He had seen the footprint of a yeti in the snow. He later explained that yeti is a mythical creature which is said to be living in the snowy mountains. Nobody has ever actually seen one in the wild, only his footprints. Bidyasagar was getting curious to know more about a Yeti.

Once everyone left, he found the sherpa to be alone. He walked towards him and asked more about the Yeti. The sherpa told him he has magical powers, nobody has ever seen a yeti in the white wilderness. He is very much shy of humans. He is said to be very mysterious, living alone in those snowy peaks. He was fascinated by the story. He decided he would go to these mountains, and find a Yeti. Finally, he had found a place to go. It will be a completely new landscape for him. He asked the sherpa the way to the great mountains and the next day he was on his way.

3
Yeti: The snowman

It took him a month to reach the high mountains. After climbing for days he reached one of the mountain villages. He was fascinated by the new landscape. There was snow as far as eyes could see. The white landscape had stolen his heart. He promised himself to become a poet here and also find the mysterious snowman. He feels yet again and again that he would find something here which will turn him into a revered poet. There are only two things which could turn a person into one and those are experiences in life and beauty. It could be extreme at both ends. It could be extreme good experience or a bitter one. He had gained all the bitter experiences in his life but his heart told him something magical will take place in these mountains which would change his life forever.

He got a room in one of the houses which hadn't been used by anyone for years. It was a wooden cottage and a lonely place. There was nothing but snow. He had even bought the local dress from a sherpa. He was very excited for his journey ahead. He needed someone to make him familiar to the place. There was a kid in the village who was very enthusiastic about his arrival. The kid came over and began interrogating him. The child said, "I have never been outside this village. Tell me how the world outside is?"

Bidyasagar could have said the truth that life is cruel but instead he said, "Life is wonderful out there. This place too is beautiful."

"There is nothing but snow here," the child whined.

"That's the beauty of it," Bidyasagar said. He further added, "You should love this place."

The kid said, "Yes, I love this place but I want to be a wanderer like you. It's boring to live at one place all the time." Bidyasagar simply smiled.

In the morning he could see the kid playing in the snow. Bidyasagar thought childhood is what makes this life beautiful. Earth would have been an ugly place if there were no children. There are so many things to do when we are a little kid but when we grow up boredom catches us like flu. The flu of boredom has spread throughout the human civilization. He has been a king and known how boredom spares none, not even a king. He always feels a need to go for journeys as they kill boredom for a while. Our whole life is about staying one step ahead of the boredom. Childhood is the period when boredom is at its lowest. He found it soothing looking at the child playing out in the snow. His innocence lit up his heart. He wished he could again begin life, become a kid again. He would not be a hunter but something else. He has grown fond of that child, Vishwas, a week after he came to know his name. The kid was curious regarding the authority of god. He meditated early every morning sitting on a rock and motivated Bidyasagar to do so too but something stopped him from doing it. Vishwas was curious to know more about the spiritual realm of soul.

Sometimes Bidyasagar also played with the kid. He felt good at times in the evenings when he sat on his chair and sipped his favorite mahua which he had carried all the way from his native place. He cannot live without it. He thinks about meeting the Yeti. He thinks of his beloved princess. She would have been very happy to be here with him. They could have lived an ordinary life here in the snowy mountains. This was life; we see hundreds of dreams, of which some come true. They could have lived here forever. He could spend only few months with her and feels lonely without her. Life is so cruel, or he has been too cruel to life.

Vishwas walked in the house and sat at the chair as usual. Bidyasagar asked him to teach him how to meditate. The kid said, "There are so many masters of meditation here, I am just a kid."

But Bidyasagar could feel the purity in his heart. He said, "No, I want to learn from you."

Vishwas began giggling. "You want to make me your master but you have to take me out for a week sometime." Bidyasagar agreed.

In the mornings after, Vishwas would come and teach him. Whenever Bidyasagar closed his eyes, the face of the dead monk haunted him. Vishwas could see he could not keep his eyes closed for long. Bidyasagar said, "I think I won't be able to do it, kid."

Vishwas's next words hit Bidyasagar hard. "There is nothing a man cannot do. You need to make peace with the past."

"How do I do that?"

"By paying attention to your breaths."

Still he could not close his eyes for a minute. Vishwas said, "Come, we will go for a walk in the high mountains."

Both left for the peak. Bidyasagar knew reaching a peak is the most difficult thing to do. It looks beautiful from far, these peaks, but reality is very harsh. Climbing a mountain was one of the toughest things he ever did while the kid did it with ease. He showed him techniques to climb the high peaks. Vishwas said, "Climbing the peaks of past is like climbing this peak, it's hard but you are capable."

Bidyasagar said after climbing for half an hour, "No, it can't be done by me, climbing any of the peaks. It's not for me." He was yelling by this point. Vishwas urged him to keep trying. By noon, they reached the peak. Vishwas laughed and said, "See, you can."

Bidyasagar began crying, looking down at the village. He told him the truth that he has killed a monk in the forest few months back. Vishwas went silent. Bidyasagar pleaded him to talk but he remained silent. Bidyasagar thought after a while that he should have not told the kid.

Vishwas spoke after a moment, "It's the worst thing we could do but I can see you are really sorry. There is no doubt, you have committed a great crime but still I see hope in your eyes. I will not tell this to anyone but promise me you would not harm anybody else."

Bidyasagar said he would not harm anybody without a reason and hugged him.

The kid joked, "I thought you were going to kill me."

Bidyasagar said, "I am grateful to you, kid."

They began walking down the mountain to their village. Bidyasagar laughed freely. Vishwas could feel the change in his smile. He could feel a caged bird has been set free. It's beautiful when a man walks out of the cage.

Vishwas was thinking, *I would have never come with him to the top if I would have known the fact before but now I don't fear this man. I witnessed the most beautiful sight of all time, a man's freedom from the evil cage.* Vishwas believed Bidyasagar when he said he would never harm anybody, not even an ant. Vishwas thought how this person had put faith in him and confessed everything. *I would never betray this man, I would tell nobody.* They reached the village just before the sunset. Vishwas walked back to his home and Bidyasagar sat on his chair outside his house. He could feel a peace settle within him like never before. For him the dead monk was his master and the god, the god whom he killed out of his greed. He has his redemption from greed after killing the monk.

Many thoughts were dancing in the barren field of his mind. He slept peacefully that night after a long time. He had not slept since a month. In the morning, Vishwas arrived. He found Bidyasagar sleeping peacefully. He waited for him to wake up. When he did, he was astonished to find the kid sitting next to him.

Vishwas suggested they should meditate. They sat on a rock, he was able to close his eyes and feel his passing breaths. He found it very peaceful. He felt relived. The dead monk was not haunting his thoughts. He had made peace with himself.

Vishwas had helped him achieve something which he thought he would never get in his life: Peace with the dead monk. He sat in the evening on the chair with a white sheet of paper and his thoughts. He began scribbling on the blank paper, the memories of past kept emerging from the surface of sea like an iceberg. He gave immense importance to memories. There, beneath the top of mind, lays an undercurrent flowing in every heart. He could feel sorrow deeply integrated with life but the flowers of hope should never be burnt even if the flowers have gone dry. This he learned from the monk's writing. Lost in these thoughts, he began scribbling these verses.

> The little moments of islands,
>
> Keep drifting in the blank space.
>
> They free float like water hyacinth
>
> On the top
>
> But the undercurrent of hope
>
> Shakes the root of the universe.
>
> Blizzard wind blowing
>
> In the white landscape of sorrow
>
> Covers the hill of joy with white snow.
>
> Time is a substance-less glue
>
> Which sticks the present with past
>
> And past with future,
>
> All glued together,
>
> They are inseparable
>
> Like fishes are to water.

Soon he began writing another verse. Thoughts were flowing into his head like a river. He could remember the serenity which the nature provided him. The mystery of nature has features of ghosts; it adds sparkling to the dark matter inside you. Love tends to consume the mass of nothingness. As the friction adds fire to the falling meteorite, love adds fire to the life. Life starts dazzling in the presence of love. He thinks love should be celebrated and even the friction that one feels in love should be a matter of celebration. He began writing another poem on love.

Love burns up you like friction

Does to a falling meteorite,

The ash of the stony bones of sky

Throws out smoke of joy,

But when it gets over the burning,

It leaves small fragments of nothing

But what should be celebrated is the friction

Of a body to its shadowy spirit.

His imagination was growing. He could feel the birth of a poet in him. There was still something he was missing; something which will make his thoughts complete and his heart to bloom into a heart of a poet. He knew he must find a yeti before he returns to Nalanda. Everything looked magical in the mirror of wild imagination. He wrote down his last poem of the day.

In the landscape of my thought,

Its winter,

My bodies of thoughts are wearing thick leather coats

Like one wore by Eskimos.

The snow has spread all over my thinking space,

It is very cold inside,

All the warmth has escaped.

The bears of imagination have gone for hibernation under the snow,

They will come out in spring

Till then there will no grass in the meadow,

There will be no river flowing,

Everything is frozen,

Even the windy memories.

I often think

To let go the storm

Until then I should be taking shelter in some

Wooden cabin with a chimney,

Burning heaps of dry wood.

Further, I want to raise my little dreamy lambs

But people advise me to wait for the spring.

I would have love to agree with them

Only if I would have known what to do with this chilling winter afternoons

And evenings.

I need to go,

Out in the snow

Looking for a place to build up my ranch.

In the poem he describes the landscape of inside. Everything is frozen, from dreams to memories. He is advised by everyone to wait for spring but he is too restless. He wants to go out even in the snow to discover his self.

He thought this is the time to begin his search for the Yeti. He put up a tent near the peaks. It is said Yetis find themselves at home on these peaks. It was a wild night. He was lying inside his tent. He felt something moving in the dark and thought it to be a Yeti. In excitement, he walked out without thinking. He came across a snow leopard eye to eye. He had not expected this creature roaming out. It began to walk away finding a human. The snow leopard was curious but did not stop there for long to shed his curiosity. Bidyasagar ran behind the snow leopard but it got lost in the dark. He was not equipped enough to follow the animal further.

The snow leopard looked at him in the dark in a strange way. Bidyasagar felt it was inspecting the tent. It could have easily attacked him but instead it got away, lost in the dark.

In the morning, he woke up late. The sun was shining. The weather looked good. He decided to walk down to the village which would take him the whole day but his ration was going to get over. He realized he needed more if he had to spend a week here. He began walking thinking of the snow leopard. It took hours to reach the village. Vishwas was playing in the snow as usual. He called out to him and asked him about the Yeti. Vishwas asked, "Why do you want to know about the Yeti?

Bidyasagar jokingly said, "I have come to find it."

Vishwas began laughing. "We have been living here from years but we have not come across any Yeti. We have only seen his footprints.

"What did his footprints look like?"

Vishwas made a large footprint in the snow. It was much larger than a human foot. A Yeti footprint could be easily distinguished from a normal human footprint.

Bidyasagar asked, "Are you sure?"

"Tell nobody," said Vishwas, "but I discovered its footprints once when I was out playing very far away from the village. It looks similar to what I have drawn. Yetis are nocturnal. It is always at night one can find them." By the time he finished, his mother was calling him. He went home. Bidyasagar rested in the house for the night. He left for the peak after his daily meditation the next day. He took help of three people to carry his food for a week. The three people rested in the tent with him that night and in the morning left for the village.

Bidyasagar was alone now. Winter was about to get over but here in these peaks, snow is perennial. He was thinking where to begin. It has been a month and there was no sign of the Yeti. He badly wanted to find it. Few days passed. He did not find anything out there. He began enjoying his solitude. He thinks all the time about his life, about yeti, about his beloved princess, about death. There was beauty in everything. That night Bidyasagar was sitting and reading inside his tent. He again felt as if there was something out there. He stepped out but there was nothing except the footprints of a snow leopard. Next night he again spotted the snow leopard. He was not able to understand why the leopard came over every day. There must be a reason, he thought. It must be the food, he thought and slept.

He remembered the footprints of yeti in his head. Another month passed but he could not find yeti. He was getting weary. He doesn't want to walk back without meeting the yeti. One night again he felt something. He didn't walk out thinking it would be the snow leopard. Next morning when he stepped out, he was surprised to see the footprints of yeti. He began cursing himself. If he could have walked out, maybe he would've spotted what he had been waiting for. It was gone now, only his footprints remained. He took the measurement of the footprint. It was almost similar to what Vishwas had shown him. He was frustrated with himself. He was cursing that snow leopard who arrived every night and disturbed his sleep. If the snow leopard had not been there, he must have looked out.

Few days passed but there was no sign again. But the snow leopard was seen again and again. There was something mysterious about the leopard. He was always there in the night near his tent, inspecting something. He decided to track the snow leopard footprint to know the place of its residence. As usual the leopard was back on time; at midnight it arrived and began circling the tent. He got an intuitive feeling that the leopard would help him out to reach the yeti. He kept following the footsteps of the snow leopard. He was astonished the speed these leopards ran in the snowy terrain. To his astonishment, he found a strange shift in the footprints of the snow leopard. From a point, the footprint of the snow leopard changed into a large footprint of human-like feet. He could not believe his eyes. The footprints changed their form and there were no other prints. If a man walked this way, there should have been two footprints, one of the leopard and other of the man. Further, the footprint was similar what he had seen a night before near his tent. It was strange the way footprints changed. It appeared the snow leopard changed into a Yeti. This was just a wild speculation but the evidence supported it.

His next move was to keep looking for the snow leopard. He began to think maybe it is the Yeti who arrives every night near his tent in the form of a snow leopard. Several questions began rising in his mind. Weather every snow leopard is a Yeti in disguise or few Yetis takes the form of snow leopard to hide themselves from the human eyes. There were more and more questions but no answers. He decided to solve the mystery. For days there no snow leopard was seen. It appeared the yeti knew someone was aware of its secrets.

One fine evening, the sun had set hours ago. Bidyasagar was walking in the snow. He heard something far away. It was a snow leopard. Both stopped, they looked at each other like previous times they had. Neither of them moved. The snow leopard stood quietly at its place. Bidyasagar thought it could be a Yeti. There was no way he could ask the snow leopard to turn into one and show him. When the snow leopard began walking away, he said quietly, "I know you are a yeti who has been following me for a month now. I will do you no harm. I want to talk to you." The snow leopard smiled and walked away. In the wildness, Bidyasagar ran behind him as fast as he could but soon the leopard was gone.

He was puzzled whether that was a snow leopard or a yeti. His mind was getting heavy with questions. He began thinking of a reason the snow leopard did not react. After a while, he concluded it must be the language. Next time when he came across the leopard few days later, he shouted in native language, *I know it's you.* The leopard stopped. It began walking towards him. Bidyasagar was terrified. Suddenly it changed into a man-like figure but much larger than an average human. It was indeed a Yeti and he couldn't believe his eyes. The yeti said, "Why are you looking for me so desperately? Nobody has ever seen me; you are the first one to see me." Bidyasagar was astonished to hear him speak fluently.

"Do you speak?"

The yeti laughed and said, "What you think I am doing, kid? And you were wrong, I know your language too."

"I am a grown man," complained Bidyasagar.

"You are just a kid to me. I have inhabited this place for centuries. I am 300 years old, kid."

Bidyasagar could not believe it. *300 years.*

"We live for over 1000 years. Why were you looking for me?"

"I have few questions only you could answer. Why do you run away from humans?"

The yeti said, "I will tell you a story. Listen to the story and you will get your answer."

4
The Story

"Thousands of years back, humans and yetis lived together. There was peace and harmony between them. We lived like animals. We were wild spirit. We walked in the wilderness like brothers. We ate raw flesh, had nothing to do but wander in the wilderness for food and enjoy nature. It felt good to be a friend to humans. We had no possessions which belonged to us. There was no selfishness among us. We hunted together and got our food. Soon humans began forming settlements and wanted to acquire material. The materialistic age had just begun. The place where humans live now was a beautiful forest once. A beauty compared to nothing. Humans found iron and formed an axe out of it. They began cutting down the forest. The yetis tried to stop them, tell them how they would ruin it, but they didn't listen.

Soon the beauty disappeared. Man began creating their own world leaving the wilderness. We Yeti decided we would live in the wild as we have been living for millions of years. We wanted to live in nature not away from it. We were against the idea of a separate isolated world. Soon humans and yeti turned into enemies. The yetis got lost in the crevices of time but we remained alive in the human consciousness. No man ever saw us again. They began believing in the nonexistence of us. We faded from the human memory but it was retained in a part of their memory. That's why they still believe in us. They look for us. Few centuries later, a yeti discovered we have magical powers, we could take the form of any beast. We could have attacked humans and could have avenged but we have seen human history very closely. This would not have brought peace but more wars. In human world, wars have become a new normal but it is the ugliest thing. We decided to live in the wild in the form of a snow leopard to escape any conflict with the humans. We have been living peacefully since then. We are very much happy and satisfied in our lives. We have seen you growing from a wild animal to a social animal then into a political one. You can't live together, even two of your species. There is a possibility there would be conflict if even two humans are left on the whole planet. You want everything to happen according to your will. You want to replace gods with yourself.

We know the day there would no uncertainty left and you could read the future, you would claim the empire of heaven. You would go to wars with gods. You have no respect for Mother Nature, the mother who has birthed you. We still believe in nature as our mother. You abandoned your mother long back. Yours is a selfish species and you care for nothing but self-growth. You have achieved every material luxury but still the road of happiness is far from your reach. And it's only getting farther. You are caught in the grip of sadness. I have visited your cities; they are nothing but heap of rocks. We could sense future you would grow into a highly intellectual breed that would never be satisfied and happy. Your cities would be materialistically rich but your soul would get poorer and poorer. That is your destiny. You have a gift of selfishness; this would help you attain magical powers without the natural gift of magic. We could see you turning a hill into a road. Soon you would be able to talk to people miles away. You would travel in transportation of great speed equal to light.

We can predict the life you would be living. It would be a life away from nature, in isolated artificial pockets. We would never abandon Mother Nature. One day there would be a great war between humans and yetis. War is the last thing we want but I fear it would happen in future. We know we may be defeated but we will die fighting for nature. No amount of materialistic progress would bring happiness to your breed. Humans were once a very happy species. You were never so sad. But depression and anxiety would grip your population and then you will run towards nature for solace, but by then nature would have disappeared. You will turn this world into an ugly place. The future is strictly based on the conditions of present. There would be skyscrapers everywhere, you would be in the space, you would even reach mars but the closer you will walk towards the materialistic god, the farther you would get from real gods.

Happiness would become a rare virtue in your breed but a yeti? He would be happily living his life in the wilderness. We roam in the night looking at the majestic nature. We have also evolved; once we were living in forest but there was lot of human intrusion although some yetis still live there. The remote cold landscape was among the place where humans didn't walk. We came here in these mountains to live peacefully. For centuries we did but then you grew in number and began to inhabit these high mountains too. These peaks along with remote wilderness are the only place where we could find solitude. In coming years we would go homeless. The way you are growing, you would cover everything. In the future centuries, the world will be a lot different. These peaks would be intruded space; we would still be living around you in the form of snow leopards. We will be only few thousands left but your population would be in billions. There would never be such an unhappy species ever. I can see the life you would be living. There would be inequality, war, violence and bloodshed everywhere. This is your destiny."

Bidyasagar was hypnotized by the tale. He listened without interrupting the yeti.

"I can see humans reduced to materialistic slaves. You would enslave even your own beings; you will always be divided. Greed and selfishness would never let you unite. They would be background evils dwelling in every human space. They would go with you wherever you go. You would be modern demons in the future. You would be demons for the all other forms of life. You would be your own demon too.

The inequalities would be disturbing. There would be horrific wars which would destroy everything. The world is heading towards destruction. Species after species would go extinct; you would laugh on their dead piles. You would crown yourself with more and more greed.

Yetis can't see their own future, that's our curse but we can see the future of others. We accept everything with grace. The other thing which we hate about humans is your ingratitude. You are not thankful to anything. You want more and more, a never-ending cycle runs your world. We realized humans are a threat to the Yeti world. It's turning out to be true; last month I saw a dead snow leopard. It was not a yeti, but it was our brother. There would be more such deaths of innocent creatures. We may go extinct but we would die defending Mother Nature till our last breath. A great war is coming between humans and the yetis.

"I talked to you because last night while you slept, I read your poems. It was fascinating. I liked your views about the world. Every yeti is a poet. If you had not been a poet, I wouldn't have spoken to you. Anyway, that's enough serious talk. Tell me a poem tomorrow. You know the future now. I would meet you tomorrow night."

The yeti walked away. Bidyasagar was mesmerized. He sat on a rock thinking everything the Yeti had told him. He felt his world was really beautiful. In these peaks, life could be harsh but there is beauty in every inch of snow. The yeti was right, once the whole world would have been beautiful. Humans are turning it into garbage and the future didn't look too bright. He could imagine the place it would become after hundreds of human induced world wars. He wrote, sitting there on the rock.

Bidyasagar had witnessed wars and knew the ugliness they brought. That ugliness and futility of war began flowering into a poem.

Once upon a time,

In the kingdom of rhymes.

There were few words

Which were sharp like swords.

They were always in fight,

The words echoed every night

From the heart of wilderness.

Look beyond the blue surface,

The sun always shines.

You need it more when you move up in alpines.

The word which were in battle,

Were peace and war.

The words which were in battle

Were Arabian Sea and the Thar.

Most of us love peace but few love war.

Most of us love island on Arabian Sea, few love the desert Thar.

Peace paints the wall white, war turn it red.

Thousands and thousands of fathers are dead

In their grave.

They were naïve and brave.

Why we love swords more than flowers.

I sat and saw the world from war towers.

The world was burning in flames.

War is nothing but rich people's games

To save their empire,

From the neighbor's fire.

In war man is defeated by man.

The sight of redness turns my heart barren.

The battle between war and peace will go on,

Until a new world is born,

Where Siddhartha is the ruler.

That world will be beautiful,

A world without guns, a world without dictators.

His head was getting heavy with thoughts. He decided to pen down another poem. Everything was coming from the mind freely. He was not putting any friction to his thoughts. He wrote the second poem after having a walk in those mountains. He walked downward towards the little woods where the red flowers were glowing on the green cheek. There were few birds chirping. Hours later, this moment took the shape of words.

I walked and joy followed me like my pupil,

I found a hermit living in me,

On the corner of mind.

I walked, some of the red flowers of tall trees

Had fallen down on the ground,

I felt I am staring at some sketch

Painted in red by the great Vincent van Gogh.

I wanted him to capture

The fallen beauty from the branches of grace

But still it had same glory

Left in its bright blazing petals.

Birds were sitting on the branches

As the trees were temples,

They were singing to the god

Their little song with a devotion which lack

In humans in general,

Each bird was making music becoming Tansen or Mozart.

Their song had silenced the agony of universe,

All birds made me feel,

This is the only way to live,

Live with gratitude towards the almighty,

Towards the dazzling sun,

The source of all life.

The birds were like detached soul

Trapped in poor body uttering out

Words of Kabir.

These were two poems he wrote for the yeti. The yeti listened to them with interest. He liked them. The only thing that would be a savior in the artificial world would be art. It will keep humans a little closer to their self. This is one thing yetis and humans have in common, they love art of all forms.

The yeti and Bidyasagar became good friends. Both would recite their poems to each other. Bidyasagar had found a friend in the form of yeti, a friend for which he was looking since a long time. The yeti told him more about the future and of the glorious past. He wrote a poem on the snow leopard. They have been their companion in the wild. They are inspired by the lives of snow leopards.

Snow leopard

Here, there are no footprints of smoke

In these snow-covered rocks.

Standing alone on the edges of these steep slopes

Reunites my heart with lost hope.

The wind here is thinner than paper

But it not flatters,

The eternal silence stops the continuous chatter

Of the mind,

It is this place where one finds

Life is tough, it's not kind.

This white solitude is my nest

Where I dwell and rest.

Here exists no one other than me

Not a beast or a bird.

I am the king of these high mountains,

I am a snow leopard.

Days passed, he lived on the peak for a month. Every night the yeti would accompany him in the snowy walks. The sky will remain filled with twinkling stars. Bidyasagar told yeti about Nalanda. "It's a majestic place to be, I would be going back to Nalanda. This time I hope I pass the test. I would abandon my material life. I would not go for greed."

The yeti warned him it is a very difficult thing to do. Lust and greed will try to push you away from the paths you want to walk. "I will try my best," said Bidyasagar, "to walk on the right path." Yetis and humans were again friends that night. That night when he was sleeping, the monk walked into his dreams. He said, "I am not dead, I am inside you. I will be living in you. You have cherished me very well. Return to Nalanda. That was the place I wanted to visit but you ended my journey in that forest." The monk smiled and disappeared.

Bidyasagar woke up from the dream, half in sweat. Nalanda was calling him. Next night, he walked to the rock where he and the yeti often met. The yeti asked, "You are leaving in a week?"

Bidyasagar said, "Yes, time has come for us to part our ways. We might meet again, my friend." The yeti turned into a snow leopard and disappeared into the wilderness, the king of mountains gone to look after his empire.

Bidyasagar walked to the village in the afternoon. He went to the house where he had been staying. He decided he would leave in a week for Nalanda. Spring has graced the mountains. Few birds arrived at his doorstep from the forest. He sat on the chair with his chilled mahua. He was thinking if he would be allowed this time, he would pass the test. He has learnt the art of poetry quite well. He has even read the medicinal books again. He hoped this time he would not be asked to walk back. Rejection is a bitter experience for anyone. Nobody wants to be rejected in either love or war. He had a good time in those mountains. He called Vishwas and told him the wild stories but didn't mention the yeti because he asked him not to reveal his existence to the world.

He said to Vishwas, "I have to take you on a little trip. It has been due for a long time. We would leave for Karnika." It was a place where Vishwas could get wings to his imagination.

Vishwas was very excited to explore the jungles of Karnika. It would delay his departure to Nalanda but he had promised him. They began early morning. After a day they reached Karnika. The forest welcomed them with their spring eyes. Bidyasagar said, "I have a jungle story for you. Long back in the jungle of Karnika, there were born hundreds of caterpillars. This is not a story of every caterpillar but of Swarnavo. Everybody played with Swarnavo. Swarnavo was a star kid among the world of caterpillars. It was said he would be the best butterfly in future. His parents remained happy; Swarnavo will do wonder once he has grown up into a butterfly. Many claimed he would be the biggest butterfly this jungle has ever seen. There was talk of his size in the jungle. He felt blessed. Then something unexpected happened. Time passed, every caterpillar turned into a butterfly except Swanavo. Every caterpillar had grown wings; they flew high in the sky but not Swarnavo. He sat wriggling on the ground. Months later the butterfly doctor said Swarnavo is suffering from a rare disorder. He would never turn into a butterfly. This broke Swarnavo's heart. Everybody got lost in their world of butterflies and Swarnavo felt deserted and abandoned. He was left alone on the forest floor to crawl. Everybody made fun of him. *See, there goes the fattest caterpillar.* Swarnavo was growing in size but there appeared no chances that he would turn into a butterfly. He felt depressed most of the time when he saw his friends flying high in the sky. He also wished two wings from the great lord. He felt god was not kind to him. He cursed his fate. His parents also began to doubt he would ever fly. Being a butterfly is every caterpillar's dream. The dream has been lost forever. He sat all day on a leaf and stared at the empty sky. He seldom talked to anyone. He felt he was good for nothing. He could see no purpose of his life. He wanted to run away from his house. Every night when he entered the gates of his house he felt like he has been a failure. There must be something he could do, he thought.

One day he was sitting as usual on a leaf. A dragonfly visited him. 'You are a mighty caterpillar. You will turn into the biggest butterfly anybody has ever seen. You will have the greatest wings.'

Swarnavo said with sadness, 'I have a curse, I would never change into a butterfly. I will remain a caterpillar my entire life.'

'No that can't be true,' said the dragon fly, 'there must be some way to beat the disorder which you are suffering from. There has to be a way.' After a long time somebody had spoken to Swarnavo with such kindness.

'I am remembering something; somewhere two butterflies were talking about your size. You must be that wonderful caterpillar. We must visit the doctor beetle who has a cure for almost everything.' Swarnavo had never heard of doctor beetle. His clinic was far off in the jungle. He could not wriggle till the place. After thinking for a moment, the dragonfly said, 'I would take you there.' It brought a twig and asked Swarnavo to hold onto it. The dragonfly tried flying carrying Swarnavo on that twig. He fell at numerous occasions but he got the balance at last. They flew to the clinic where doctor beetle examined Swarnavo for an hour.

He said, 'You lack citric acid in your body. This could be cured if you could taste lemons.

Swarnavo said, 'What the hell is a lemon?'

'It's a fruit which is found far in the east of forest. It is a very far off and distant place inhabited by humans. There is danger at every step.'

Swarnavo said, 'No matter how hard it may be, I would go there.'

The dragonfly said he would take him there. They began their journey to the lemon tree.

The sun was about to set, they took shelter in a leafy cave. It was the land of spiders. Spiders were the most dangerous creatures known to them. They could swallow their bones and dissolve the body of any insect. In the middle of the night they felt something moving towards them. It was a Tarantula. Both began running out of the leafy cave. Dragonfly could have flown away but it did not leave Swarnavo. He waited for him, risking his life. Swarnavo finally took hold of the twig and they flew away from the territory of the spiders.

The sun had begun to rise. It appeared lovely sitting on the branches of sunflower and witnessing the rising sun. It was a liberating moment. The lemon tree was still three days away. They tasted the nectar of a wildflower. It was really good.

They took off again. It began to rain heavily. The dragonfly's wings got drenched in the rain. They had no choice but to take shelter in the trunk of a tree. They waited for few hours when the sun finally came out of the cloudy cocoon and shone like a yellow diamond. The wings of the dragonfly were now dry and they left for the lemon tree. This time, a storm stopped their way. They hid in the root of a hollow tree. The storm passed after few hours. Few days later they finally reached the lemon tree. Swarnavo tasted as much lemons he could. Soon a man came with a can of chemical and began sprinkling it on the lemon tree. Few drops fell on Swarnavo but they managed to escape unhurt. Swarnavo took a lemon with him.

After few days, magic happened. Swarnavo turned into a butterfly. He was truly the biggest butterfly one has ever seen. He began flying in the sky with his glorious wings. Everybody came to witness the great transformation. It was on the front page of the jungle newspaper. Everyone wanted to be his friend now. All came shouting *Swarnavo, Swarnavo* but he knew who his true friend was. He was aware of the fakeness. He went and hugged the dragonfly. For him, the dragonfly was the only insect that stood by him at the time of need. The struggle was long but it always pays. He was a living wonder in the forest.

Vishwas liked the story. They came across a number of wild animals. Vishwas was excited to explore the jungle. They spent a week there. Bidyasagar fulfilled his promise. He walked back to the village. He took Vishwas to his house, met everyone in the village and left for Nalanda. There were tears in Vishwas's eyes. Bidyasagar promised he would visit him again but for now, a new chapter was waiting.

5

The Doorsteps of Nalanda

After a year, Bidyasagar was again at the doorsteps of Nalanda. The guards were still there guarding the great gates. They were the same scholars who had taken his test the last time. They again asked him who he was.

"I am a poet and an Ayurveda teacher." He said.

They asked him a few questions regarding medicinal herbs. He told them the cure of every disease they asked. They were impressed. At last they asked him to write a poem on love. It took him just a few minutes and soon he was reciting it to the learned guards.

I think I know what love is,

A curse without which you cannot live

Or die,

You want it to be in your heart

Like sunrays,

Otherwise there will be no free bird

In your black sky.

Love is like the warmth of winter's sun,

Love is like Vincent van Gogh's suicidal gun.

It's like the shadow from which no one can run

But still everyone is trying to get away from it.

I want to tell everyone, it's futile

Because love is the only thing on this earth

Which make us smile.

But sometimes love could be a dreaded crocodile

Of River Nile.

Love is an anchor of a ship which keeps a man at shore

But it can set you free when you begin to bore.

Love is a treasure worth dying for,

More precious than mines of Uranium ore.

Love can be our daily chore.

Love can be heaven's secret door

And sometime love is the only thing

Which our hearts love to abhor.

Love is a pirate's secret code,

Love could be a fulcrum

Which can balance the effort and the load.

Love is a poisonous toad

Moving in the forest looking for the wild road

Which would take it on a tour of Paris.

Love is like metamorphosis.

He passed the test. His dream to walk inside the great
Nalanda monastery had come true. He was elated. When

he first stepped in, he could see the grandness of Nalanda. There was a huge monastery in the middle which was a place for prayers. One person accompanied him as a guide to his room. Tomorrow the same person will give him a tour of the place. He could see hundreds of monks and students walking across the premises of Nalanda. Soon he reached his room. It was a small with a cot and a chair. He liked the place. He was very tired from the journey and soon slept. In the morning when he woke up, he could see the gentle sunlight entering his room and lighting up the whole place. Apart from the light, gentle breeze was also passing through the room. Every structure in the monastery was unique. Bidyasagar had never seen such a place in his entire life. He could hear the hymns to Siddhartha. There were several statues of Siddhartha inside the premises. That day, he came to know more about him. He was the prince who left everything to attain peace in life. Siddhartha turned into Buddha.

He bathed in a nearby well where several other students of the monastery were bathing too. It was a paradise on earth, paradise to attain knowledge. Soon came the guy who took him for a little tour of the place. He first took him to the garden inside the premises. The man said, "Here you can look at the clear sky and think without any disturbance from anyone. In Nalanda the purpose of learning is to become a thinker. Every human should be a thinker. Thinking is the most important aspect of human life. We all should motivate our mind to think. There are thousands of questions to engage the mind and soul. The thirst should light up your spirit to explore the realm of knowledge. One must learn the art to think and question the world. Questioning is the integral part of learning without which we cannot learn.

We should question each and everything that surrounds us. Anybody who is against the art of questioning is against the art of learning. Everything in this world is subject to change. The art of question helps us to understand this change which is evident in everything. Time is the greatest mystery of all time. Here you will learn the art of thinking through the means of questioning. Speak out any question which your mind holds, shoot these questions out of the grave and give life to them."

After the garden, Bidyasagar was taken to the prayer room where everyone was offering prayer to the great soul. No one forced others to pray; you offered a prayer only if you wished to. There was a strange purity in the prayers. His companion further said, "Explore the world with your own reasoning, even prayers. I have felt offering prayers to the great lord have helped me in knowing the nature of self."

Bidyasagar was mesmerized by the beauty of the place. Within a week he was well acquainted with the greatest place of learning on the face of earth. Day after day, he spent his time in the library. It was a three-storied building. There were thousands and thousands of books in every shelf. He was lost in the crowd of books. He would read night and day about Siddhartha and the medicinal herbs. He wanted to know everything about the medicinal plants and herbs. The horizon of his knowledge was expanding day after day. He got addicted to the books. The more he read about Siddhartha, the more fascinated he became with the world. Siddhartha was his ideal; even the dead monk revered him. There were many questions rising in his little head. He has seen the power of compassion. Compassion was more powerful than thousand swords put together. Practicing compassion requires a great deal of courage. The night Siddhartha left his palace, what must he be thinking? What was that force which pushed him away from the palace? He has too lived in the palace. Life is more than senses. There is a hidden world inside us. Every human needs to explore that mysterious force. Palaces might be grand but nature is the grandest stage to be. The words of Yeti returned to his mind. Siddhartha found enlightenment under peepul tree. The tree is the symbol of nature. Siddhartha spoke of compassion to not only humans but every living creature. Nature helped him to gain that supreme knowledge. Yeti too was an enlightened living being. We all need to awaken from the great sleep. We must wake up from our hibernating self which wants the winter to never get over so it could sleep under the snow forever. No one can sleep forever; sleeping forever is death. Palaces could bring comfort to body but it is the mind which craves for peace. Every human mind looks for peace. There is no divinity in chaos, chaos has elements of darkness. People who love the chaotic form of life are the ones who crave for order the most. He wanted to talk to Siddhartha but he was dead. He could reach to Siddhartha through texts and scriptures. He also wanted to awaken himself from the hibernating self.

What was it Siddhartha was running from? It must have been the darker self. We all run from it. We want it to hide but truth could not be hidden for long. His father wanted him to be a great ruler but there is nothing wilder than one's own mind. It is essential to rule one's own mind. There are two ways to live this life: either get dissolved in the materialistic liquid and lose the essence of life or let the sediments of dust settle down in the materialistic liquid. When we burn up the material liquid, the smoke rises from the hollow bones. This smoke forms a shape in the sky, the shape of a vessel, a vessel which will never be filled. We are all like that empty vessel. Even thousands of palaces will not provide the material which the soul needs to survive, but a hut would. We have to keep our soul alive. We should not let the fire extinguish. Siddhartha realized the futility of the palace in maintaining his peace of mind. When he came across the harsh realities of life, his dream got shattered. We all knit up a nice flowery dream but life is not flowery. One has to learn the essence of life through experience. It is through the experiences he harnessed on his way to enlightenment which helped him to break the material cocoon. There is no doubt we need material to an extent to survive but making the gold more important than thoughts ruin the stability of peace. When the horses of chaos leave the stable of peace, there is a state of confusion hanging in the atmosphere. The more he came to know about Siddhartha, the more he became aloof from the worldly pleasure. He began to think he was awakened.

He began loving the place. Day after day, he would spend his time reading precious books. But everything changed when a group of dancers arrived. There she was, Smriti. The minute Bidyasagar saw her; he fell in love with the lady. Her charming beauty had an impact on him. Few days later, he saw her mesmerizing performance. He wanted to talk to her. There were numerous poets in Nalanda. One of them was Suryakanth who was a well-known poet. He saw Suryakanth reciting poetry to Smriti while they sat in the garden. That was the moment he discovered jealousy. He wanted to be there instead of Suryakanth. He wanted the dancer to be on his side.

Few days later he approached Smriti with one of his

poems. She heard him but did not seem impressed. The same day, there was a poetry competition in Nalanda. Everybody read their poems but Suryakanth came out victorious. The defeat was a harsh moment for Bidyasagar. *How he could be defeated?* The rudimentary nature of self was taking over him slowly. Everything he had read and experienced vanished. He stopped going to the library and began thinking of ways to beat Suryakanth in the next poetry competition taking place next month. He wanted to write the best poem, better than Suryakanth.

The more jealous he felt, the worse his writing went. He was not able to write anything. Jealousy was consuming him and his art. Suryakanth wrote excellent pieces of poems but Bidyasagar could not write a word.

He felt as if the world was coming to an end. Every day he felt worse and worse. The hunter in him awoke from the sleep. He wanted to avenge his defeat. He began planning a murder although he had promised Vishwas he would not harm anybody. Jealousy was taking away his knowledge. He had become a slave. He lost the poetry competition yet again. Smriti was in love with Suryakanth. He saw both sitting in the garden and talking night after night. Everything was fueling the fire inside him. He forgot everything: his promise, the words of the dead monk. He could have done anything to get Smriti.

The night he was about to murder Suryakanth, a strange thing happened. He was walking towards the poet's room. The night was blooming like the flowers of rajnigandha. He saw an owl looking him. There were three owls in the garden; two owls were fighting to make love to the other owl. He could see how hard they were fighting each other. He could feel the drive which was forcing both owls to tear each other apart. All the fight was merely for flesh. Suddenly, one owl left the fight and flew away in the dark. He looked at the moon and left the fight. That owl felt something and he left the quest of lust.

Bidyasagar was not able to understand why suddenly the owl had left. It had spotted something in the sky and the desire evaporated. He followed the bird which came and sat on the mango grove looking at the moon. The owl seemed mesmerized by the moon. It saw a shadow walking towards it. The shadow said, "Don't get trapped in the worldly chains. Break free, you will not get freedom in the feathery arms. I have crossed the ocean of lust by walking in the fire. The fight you are performing will give you momentarily pleasure, and then the fragrance of the body will get lost in the wind. Understand life, don't make it feel short. I am Siddhartha, I have walked the path. It's difficult but there is joy embedded in it. The joys which will make you feel free from the worldly chains. Understand the futility of the fight. Be Siddhartha, walk free in the fire, burn the barren field of dry grass of lust and desire."

Bidyasagar too heard the voice of the shadow. Suddenly everything disappeared; there was no owl, no moon in the sky, no shadow at all. He was bewildered; he could not understand if it was real or his imagination. But he understood the futility in killing Suryakanth. He began crying, he didn't know what to do. He had promised Vishwas he would never harm anybody meaninglessly. He went to the library at midnight and opened the book on Siddhartha. He understood what the shadow wanted to convey. He was back to his senses. He has been mesmerized by her beauty. He loved Smriti but he could love her in her absence.

Love is a complex organism. One does not need to have that person in life to love. Love should be freedom, not a cage. He loved Smriti but did not need her in his life. He began thinking of love, a feeling raw in nature but ripe in form, that feeling which isolates a person from the horizon of endless sky. He realized what he had been about to do, the other blunder in life by killing Suryakanth. If he would have killed him, he would not have been able to forgive himself. Siddhartha saved him. He decided he would give his life in service of treating people with his knowledge of medicine. He would write poetry in his spare time and rest all the hours of day he would spend in treating sick people. He went to the head monk of the monastery and shared his desire to treat people. Nobody could walk inside the monastery without passing the tests but the head monk allowed people to walk in for treatment on one condition: they had to immediately leave post treatment and they could not walk beyond the permitted area. If they would like to cross it, they had to pass the test like everybody else.

He no more felt jealous of Suryakanth. He had made a pact with self. He would not walk astray anymore. He has seen what jealousy could do. It could turn a naïve person into a monster. The rudimentary instincts could make a person walk astray easily. He began thinking the extent of what jealousy could do: it could burn the world. It is the most evil force produced by the mind which has self-destructive properties. He could not believe he wanted to murder someone over jealousy. He had gone blind but he got is inner eyes back at the face of consciousness. There is a very thin line between evil and good. He was able to write again. He could write like before. His head was empty of the ill-feeling. He was gaining his art back from the devil who had almost defeated him. Our negativity turns the devil into a stronger force. He needed to practice meditation more vigorously. He began meditating for hours every day. One needs continuous practice to escape the clutches of the devil. He could feel the devil shrinking in him but it never dies. It always remains there, if not active then in a dormant stage, like a seed. The fertilizer of greed, lust and selfishness turns that seed into a full-bloomed evil flower. Which will produce more seeds and soon the inner landscape of mind will turn into an evil forest. Then beasts would take birth in the darkness of that evil forest. Those beasts will grow and turn themselves into a powerful evil spirit which spell would make you weaker and weaker. That's how it begins, from just a single seed; there could be an evil forest, then evil beasts, then evil spirits, which would dilute the purity of souls with negative emotions of life. One should always be aware of the negative emotions. They are equally powerful and ignorance gives them more power. The devil tries very hard to make you sleep by playing the sad music. One gets hypnotized by the evil and the goodness begins to fade in the background.

Bidyasagar woke up early the next morning. He could hear the peaceful pleasant hymns and prayers. He decided to pray. It was the first time he had walked into the prayer room. He prayed to Siddhartha, thanking him for saving him from committing the greatest sin he could have done by killing Suryakanth. He found solace, looking at the silent statue of Buddha. He liked the place the monks were offering their prayers at. He could see the magic of prayers. Siddhartha is nothing but our greater self. We all could turn into Siddhartha, we could all achieve our greater self. Being Siddhartha is the first stage and becoming Buddha is the final stage. We first turn into Siddhartha, that wandering self, looking for that awakening experience. Buddha-hood is the final stage in our awakening self. Bidyasagar has turned into Siddhartha. He could feel that thirst for supreme knowledge. He could feel the need to awaken from the great sleep. He needs to break the hibernation of the soul. The polar bear in the landscape of thoughts needs to come out of the snow and look at the spring of life.

Soon he began treating sick people in and around Nalanda. His knowledge of medicine was helping hundreds of people every day. He could treat all serious diseases. His fame soon reached to far places. He was known Bidyasagar, the healer. He was healing the pain of the common people. He found happiness hidden in the service. In the little spare time he got, he wrote his poetry and felt that immense joy flowering within. At night, he was lost in looking at the stars. He was amazed by the fact how less we know about the outer and the inner world. He saw a comet passing across the sky; he was amazed by the beauty of the universe. Soon he befriended an astronomer friend who would tell him curious stories of space. They will spend their nights exploring the space. They would wonder if man could someday walk on the moon and Mars. There are strange stories—some say there is a palace of god on the moon, and some say footsteps of god. When a thing is far and unknown, only one thing explains it, *speculation*. We all are habituated of the speculation. His astronomer friend would say moon would be nothing but heap of dust, yet beautiful. There could be beauty in barrenness if we have the right eyes. His knowledge about life, space, medicine, everything was expanding. He could feel that expansion fueling more and more vigor to know the world. He could feel bees of happiness turning his emptiness into honey. He could taste that sweetness in himself. The desert within was turning into a wild orchard where birds chirp till late night. The mystery was unfolding slowly like blossoming of a wildflower. He sat one day and in silence and wrote poems after poems. Inspired by the monster within, he tried to write down a poem which could encompass courage in the hearts of men. He felt the presence of monster in him. The negative emotion could consume you like termites do a dry wood. Until the stream of love is flowing in the mountains of dry bones, the flowers will keep blooming.

> It is easy to let the monster win,
>
> It is easy to become some misery queen.
>
> It is easy to let the things as it has always been.
>
> It is easy to let your dreams turn into some ruin
>
> Which you cannot visit,
>
> But I will tell you what is tough,
>
> To tame the monster like some pet
>
> Who is no more than a puppet.
>
> It is tough to open the gate
>
> Of the fort of fear.
>
> It is tough to move back the falling tears
>
> In the black pond.
>
> It is tough to die for your homeland.
>
> It is tough to hold the sand
>
> Between your fingers.

It is tough to be a wild river

When a city comes next to you.

It is tough to sew

The wound without any stitches.

It is tough to distribute all the riches

You have earned by looting.

It is tough to give away the habit of shooting

The stars

With your parachute.

It is tough to hold on to the roots.

It is tough to throw away the rubber boots.

It is tough to walk without foot.

Now he believed god always gives you a hint when you are walking astray. Keep your eyes and ear open. It could be through a bird's song, through falling feather, through a passing comet. One could escape the territory of evil through his goodness. One has to be alert himself, gods will come to rescue you from the depths of hell but keep listening to the wind and the bird song. He began writing something on wet clay. The demons could not fool you until and unless you are unable to decipher the secret messages of the almighty. It is easier to blame gods and the demons for your wrong doings. One cannot run from his karma. Somewhere we all get a chance to escape but we don't choose it. Choices are always given to you. It is far easier to surrender to fate but tough to fight it. He began writing these words:

Life can never confuse you,

And demons cannot use you

Against your will.

Don't blame the demons,

Blame yourself.

You could have saved yourself from drowning in mud.

Now you think it was all the will of god

But it wasn't.

Think again.

The scene, the moment

You could have escaped

But you choose to remain dead,

The grass was green but suddenly it turned red.

Empty your lungs of stale memories and bad air,

Life is nothing but a cursed theatre,

Don't waste your morning prayers

On someone who don't care,

Of your love and sorrow.

Believe me, there can always be a better tomorrow,

How bad this moment may be,

Like a brave rabbit caught in some snare

You can also dare to dream

Even after hearing the moaning of bulbuls and those ghostly screams

Of crickets,

Dream of returning again to the burrow

Or meeting that kind sparrow

Who dwelled like some angel in your neighbourhood.

Think for a moment

Who put that bait there,

It was no one else but you.

Now you feel depressed in that snare

But dream to dare

Like that rabbit of returning back to the burrow

And meet her sparrow.

6

Metamorphosis

Sun was setting. Vikram was returning home after ploughing the fields for whole day. He was tired but he would not sleep without giving chapattis to all the dogs living in his vicinity. He was much inspired by the story and life of Buddha. He had embraced the teachings of Buddha with all his heart. There were questions which kept rising in his head like phoenix from the barren fields of mind. He reached home after giving chapattis to poor dogs, kept water out for the birds as it was summer. In the morning he would not get time to refill these empty jars with water. Last year there was a great drought, thousands of birds died. It was a horrible sight; birds were falling from the branches like twigs. Their beautiful feathers turned into dust, their skeleton were on display beneath every tree, displaying the hardship of life. Death was everywhere, cattle, people all were dying but he survived the drought. The drought ended with rain. Soon everything was green again. The dryness was covered behind green leaves. He thinks such is life; we are hit by great adversity but then wounds heal and sometimes it feels it never happened.

Vikram dreamt of Nalanda monastery, he always wanted to go there. The conditions prevailing at home never allowed him to visit the place. The drought lead to the death of two oxen he had. He had to buy a team of new oxen from the animal fair. In the evening on the way home, he sits on the grass and thinks what the purpose of his life is. He looks far in the little pond where ducks are swimming with great ease. He could see little tadpoles in the mud holes, swimming like little kings. Children think them to be little fishes. They *are* very similar to little fishes.

He remembers his childhood. Once he had brought few tadpoles home. He thought them to be baby fishes. He nurtured them with care for months. The tadpoles grew and grew and to his surprise turned into frogs. He thought he had witnessed a magic, the fishes turning into frogs. He thought similarly someday he would turn into some bird and fly away far into a jungle. He always wanted to be a bird but instead he was a man. He smiled when children caught the tadpoles and said, "Hey, I have got a little fish." May be frogs are fishes in childhood just as we are free spirits in childhood but then something happens and we turn into frogs. We no more remain fishes, our gills of imagination disappear and our happiness turns into a rough texture. Nobody knows why it happens. This is not magic; tadpoles should remain fish, the gills of imagination should not disappear but unfortunately we all end up turning into a frog.

He wanted to learn the philosophy of life. He has listened very carefully to the stories told by monks who come to the village sometimes for bhiksha. He has never visited Nalanda but has a great curiosity to go there. He wanted to know in detail how tadpoles turn into frogs. He wanted to study the metamorphosis of life. But he could not leave his old parents and pursue his learning. He has to wait until the appropriate time comes. He has been told since childhood there is a time fixed for everything. When time will come, he would get a chance to visit Nalanda. He has seen many of his fellow beings who were fishes in their childhood but now they are frogs.

He walked home with these thoughts. His father is a hard-working person. He still worked in the field whole day. He had a gift; he can see the stars and predict when it is going to rain. He had predicted the coming of great drought but nobody paid heed to him. Every night he spent his little time on the terrace looking at the stars, noting down their changing position. He had decided one day he would learn this art from his father. His father had urged him several times to go to Nalanda and he would manage the fields, but he knows there is a great deal of work here. It would be very tiring for his father. He has been very much observant like his father. He has observed there are certain birds which only visit his place in winter. In summer they fly away somewhere. He watched kingfishers catching fishes from the pond. He is very fond of birds. The birds are an imitation of the human spirit. He always wanted to know from where these birds come in winter. He wants to visit their land just as they visit his. This is unfair on god's part—they could visit his fields but he is not allowed to fly with them to their distant land.

Few months passed. One day his father got struck with high fever. The fever would not go. It was almost a week later but the fever only got stronger. He thought he would lose his father. From somewhere he came to know about Bidyasagar, that this man could save his father. He decided to visit Nalanda along with his ailing father. He arranged for a bullock cart, took his father to the cart and made him lay down. He began moving towards Nalanda. His childhood dream was about to come true but more than excitement, he was afraid. He did not want to lose his father. The ox began moving; first they had to cross the jungle. He saw a strange bird in the forest. It came and sat on the cart for a moment then flew away. He wanted to follow the bird, but he could not spare any time. He should reach Nalanda as fast as he could.

We all have to take such decisions; we want to follow our dream but we have to walk another way. He reached Nalanda in the evening. They were allowed to walk in as per the head monk's order. They went to the permitted area but found the treatment room locked. Bidyasagar has gone back to his room, they were told. His father's condition began to deteriorate and he immediately needed to go to his room but that was a restricted area. They needed to pass the test to go further. They asked a question on astronomy to Vikram on his insistence, of which he had no idea but his father was listening to the conversation between his son and the guards. He told them the answer quickly. His father's knowledge of stars paid off and they were allowed to walk in. Vikram was astonished to know how knowledgeable his father was. But without wasting any more time, he rushed to Bidyasagar's room.

Vikram greeted Bidyasagar. He told him about his father's condition. Bidyasagar checked his pulse and examined his father. He gave them few herbs and asked to wait till morning. He offered them his bed and went to the library to spend the night. In the morning when he arrived, the fever was gone. Vikram's father could walk after days.

Bidyasagar asked him how they passed the test in first attempt. Vikram told him all that happened at the inner gate, how his father's knowledge of Astronomy helped them enter Nalanda. Bidyasagar got curious how his father could predict rain.

Vikram's father, Parmeshwar, said hesitatingly, "To some extent."

"I also want to learn the art. That would be my fees." Parmeshwar said they had to return today but if he could come with them and live in their house for a month, he could teach him how to predict rain.

Bidyasagar agreed. They left with him to their village. In the jungle Vikram again spotted that bird. This time he could not resist. He said to his father, "I will be home tomorrow; I have some work in the forest." His father understood the reason behind his stay in the forest so he and Bidyasagar left for their village leaving Vikram there. His father told Bidyasagar about his son's interest in the birds and fishes.

Vikram followed the bird which had made its nest on a peepal tree. There were many such birds on that tree. One had fallen to the ground and was wounded. He picked it up and spent the night under that tree. In the morning, he left for his village with the wounded bird. He realized he would never have got this wounded bird if he wouldn't have followed his instinct.

In the afternoon, he reached his village. He saw his father was teaching Bidyasagar to sow seeds in the field. Both were laughing and enjoying themselves. He touched both his father's and Bidyasagar's feet. He showed them the wounded bird. "This bird will be my new friend. There were several similar birds on the peepal tree." He has spotted these birds in the region for the first time. They must be migratory birds.

Vikram cared for the bird as much as possible. Bidyasagar said to Vikram, "Never put this bird in a cage and it would be with you forever. Vikram listen to him. In a week the bird was healed but it was resistant to leave his house. "That's the power of compassion," Bidyasagar said. Every morning the bird would fly away but return in the evening. Vikram would wait every evening; he won't eat before offering grains to the bird. One day it didn't return. Vikram remained awake the whole night. Bidyasagar could see the eagerness in his eyes to see the bird again.

Vikram wondered if the bird had returned to its land as no one can live far from their homeland for long or it got killed by a hunter. He wanted an answer but no one could give him that. Bidyasagar said the bird will return someday and took him out for a walk.

He asked, "How do you feel about the loss?"

Vikram said, "I never thought the bird would fly away one day."

"Kid, people do leave, that's the hard fact of life. Nobody will stay with you forever. The bird might come back one day."

Vikram sighed then said, "I've had a question since a long time. Why do tadpoles lose their gills of imagination when they grow up? I have seen so many people who were tadpoles in their childhood, a tadpole which was closer to a carefree fish. Why have all ceased to be tadpoles and turned into a frog?"

Bidyasagar smiled. "That's the curse of life. You have to grow. We want our childhood back but time takes us far from the tales of childhood. I know you must be looking for the tail of a frog when they grow up but you will never find it. The little tail of childhood and the tail of tadpoles are lost. This is the ugly truth which we have to encounter. I never wanted that little tadpole in me to grow into a frog but that's how life is. You cannot find my tail but it does not mean it's not there. It's inside me. That invisible tail is still in my memories. The flower may have been lost but I hold the fragrance in me."

"What is this tail you are talking about?"

"The tales of childhood. That childhood may have been lost but those tales I still retain in my picture book of memory. The fragrance of childhood is still with me. A tadpole has to turn into a frog. Time will add that secret ingredient in you to help you grow up but as I said, the tail turns invisible with time. The people whom you see around all have their secret tails embedded deep inside their soul. It may be not visible to eyes but they can see it in the mirror of their soul."

Vikram hesitated. "Would I also turn into a frog?"

Bidyasagar smiled. "That's the fate of every living being. We all grow up but I am happy you are looking for tadpoles in the grown up frogs. I agree we lose our gills of imagination; it will get frozen in time. One has to melt time so that he can get his gills back. You need those gills because if you are a frog, it means the stream of hope will be near. Gills of imagination are needed in the river of life to survive. Most of us lose our gills of imagination but like the tail it remains inside us in a frozen form. We have to work a little hard to melt the snow and turn the glaciers into a wild river. We all have the gills and the tail of tadpoles; we just have to put an effort to bring them back from the lost world."

Vikram had his answer. Bidyasagar further told him,

"See, you are Siddhartha now; but not every Siddhartha turns into Buddha. Only few do, rest all die as Siddhartha. They die restless without knowing the final answer. It is good to be Siddhartha but one should strive to become Buddha. I could see the birth of Siddhartha in your heart but turn that Siddhartha into Buddha." He further explained the matter taking the tadpole example. "As not every tadpole turns into a frog even though it has potential, similarly not every Siddhartha end up being Buddha."

Bidyasagar had learned the basic scales of farming and the art of predicting rain. He enjoyed living with Vikram and his father but had to leave for Nalanda the next day. He asked Vikram to come to Nalanda and learn the great books in the library.

He was happy being back. On his way back to his room, he saw Smriti passing with Suryakanth.

There was no jealousy but he smiled and genuinely asked Suryakanth about his well-being. Smriti said, "There is going to be a poetry event this evening. Are you coming?" Bidyasagar told them he would. He took a bath and got ready for the occasion. That evening he wrote poetry with pure joy. He was not writing to win the competition or to impress Smriti. He felt he should write something close to his heart. The poem was on *godlessness*. It depicted the death of god. He began remembering the darker memories from his life. The cruelty he used to carry as a hunter. The anger he had against god. He thought if one thing god would allow him to take to heaven with him, he wished it would be one of his poisoned arrows to kill god. These thoughts transformed into a beautiful poem but he recalled that cruel hunter within him who wanted to kill god with his arrow. It began to rain, along with thunderbolts and lightening in the sky. He got his inspiration and started writing.

The thunder bolt lights up the sky

With a sudden rage,

But no one appears

On the black stage.

Only thing which could be seen

In fields of darkness

Is the glimpse of death.

The broken lines of brightness

Stretched on the black- blue carpet

Draws a map

Of a lost place

It is the pathway to god's grave.

It was appreciated by everyone. He won the prize, and even Smriti praised him, but he felt how futile it was to win. He was amazed he wanted so badly to win the events in the past. The joy was in writing and not winning. He decided he would never participate in any event for the sake of winning. He came back and continued writing. He was enjoying it like never before. The joy took him close to paradise. He wrote another poem sitting quietly in the garden.

I often visit the museum of past, the skully space

Which has a roughness and luster

Which time has given it.

The rust eaten antique moments

Are dancing like flame or shadow

In the black walls moving in the empty socket.

Sometimes when we put a skinny curtain

Over it,

Then things become clearer, more lucid

And the images kept in glass boxes

Become lively like the grasshoppers

And jump in the space

Where nothing exists in its truer form.

There is some past

And some future mixed in the present

Like human dreams.

Few days later, Smriti came looking for Bidyasagar. She wanted to ask him something. Bidyasagar was with a patient. She went inside and asked, "Are you free?" He wanted to say yes but he was not; there were many more people waiting for the treatment. "Can we meet in the garden at night?" She then asked and Bidyasagar agreed.

By night, he had treated all the people who had come to him. He bathed and walked towards the garden. His heart was beating fast. He was excited to meet Smriti. She was already there.

She said, "I have found a change in you since the last time we met, a change I wished to see in myself but I am unable to do that. How did you make it happen in such a short span of time?"

"What kind of change are you talking about?" he asked.

"A change which can bring a change in your aura," she said.

"I have changed a little, I know." Bidyasagar told her everything about the episode of jealousy. "I am now at peace with myself."

She was astonished to know that. "I am confused about love. I love Suryakanth but have feelings for you as well."

Bidyasagar could not understand anything. He asked, "Can you articulate?" She bluntly refused and said she felt good talking to him.

She asked, "Are you an atheist?"

"No. There was a time when I was but now I am in his service. This life of mine is his gift to me. He has shown me a way through the darkness. I was lost in an evil world. I had to kill him so that I could born again. I have witnessed my own resurrection from the ruins of hell." She liked him even more then. There was a mystery in his words.

"How do you get these beautiful words?"

"I find them from within my soul. We all have treasures hidden inside but it is we who never look inside, in the heart for these treasures. We pass our life dwelling on the colours but we never try to reach the fragrance. I have found that treasure within me; I have walked all the way, good and evil. I could say with my experience, it's always better to choose the good in you.

There must be a treasure inside your heart. You have to reach that treasure passing through the wild roads. The journey demands sacrifice. This is a virtue one always needs in his life to achieve the treasure. We all have to sacrifice our evilness to touch the silver lining of goodness. Sacrificing evil is the toughest thing to do but I did it. It took everything from me but the gift which I received put seeds of joy in my orchard of heart. The bees of joy keep buzzing in my little heart."

She liked everything Bidyasagar told her. She had to leave sometime later but he felt a strange peace after speaking his heart out. He confessed his jealousy and he felt good. He realized confession always helps a lost soul. The feelings were getting complex. He did not want to be the greatest poet; he just wanted to be a poet who writes because he loves writing. Thoughts come to him like sea urchins who want to explore the sea floor. He wants to be poet who writes for self and not for the world, most of the time he has written for the world. He discovered his desire for anonymity. He was known all over Nalanda as a great poet and great Ayurveda master. Everybody knew him. His poetry was far more popular than him. He had gained everything a person wishes for. His fame was unparalleled, even Suryakanth could not match up to it. He practiced Ayurveda for free and treated thousands of people.

7
Bakhtiyar Khilji

Bakhtiyar Khilji was at the doorsteps of Nalanda. He wanted to carve an empire for his master. The cruelty of the Turkish general was well known. He would kill anybody who did not compile with his law. He had won several war battles and was now here. He was stationed in Bakhtiyarpur, a small village named after him almost 50 kms from the monastery. He had arrived in Magadha region with 20,000 soldiers.

He walked the common village on the roadside, attracted by the buzzing life in the common streets in the region. He trusted nobody, not even his closest aid. He believed in the theory *we are dust with a purpose*. He knew it well there was an anarchy existing in the backyard of every kingdom. Magadha was a strong empire in the past but it disintegrated years ago. Every kingdom is suspicious of the other. The rules of kindness do not apply in politics of the kingdoms. He has been betrayed in the past by his closest commander once, although he managed to hold the empire but it was a lifetime lesson for him to remember.

He knew it very well. We are nothing but heaps of dust and there is a purpose assigned to every life. His purpose was to be the greatest warlord. He was not a king but not less than a king either. He has always done what he wants.

He organizes bloody fights every day to make his army brutal and cruel. Cruelty was his ideal in life. He believed in the simple fact: cruelty was a key virtue needed in this cruel world to achieve something. He was not fond of reading; rather he was fond of wars and battles. According to him, it's the weak that spend their time in such luxuries. A warrior should be always with weapons not with books. He was fond of horses. He has the finest of the horses in his stables.

But a deadly disease has taken hold of him, leaving him with limited time. He had tried every hakim in his empire but all have said they could do nothing to save him. When there is little time left one becomes kind but he was crueler. He only had few more years but he wanted to be the greatest warlord. It required sacrifices and he sacrificed everything for it.

Then, he heard of Bidyasagar and sent his men in search for him. Bidyasagar arrived upon hearing a life was in danger. Khilji was extremely jealous of people from other civilizations. He had no respect for them. He believed his race was superior. He called Bidyasagar just to check how good he was. Either he was as good as people said he was in the area or it was just a boasting by the local people. Bidyasagar arrived in Khilji's tent while he sat reading the Quran.

He asked, "Are you Bidyasagar?" Bidyasagar nodded. He told him his medical history and the condition. "I will die in few years. I want you to treat me if possible but I won't take any of your medicine." He made it clear it was a challenge and Bidyasagar accepted it.

Bidyasagar began thinking of a way to treat Bakhtiyar

Khilji. It seemed almost impossible that he could do anything without the medicines, after all, it's the medicines which treat a patient not the hakim. He again visited him and found him turning the pages of holy Quran that day as well. He observed one peculiar thing about Bakhtiyar Khilji—he had a habit of wetting his fingers with saliva by touching his tongue while turning the pages. An idea sprang into his mind. He sneakily applied the medicine on the pages of the Quran. Every day he would repeat this process and there won't be a day when he would not read his Quran. He was very strict with the schedule, thereby consuming the medicine on time. His condition began improving. He was feeling relived from the continuous pain which had been a part and parcel of his life for a long time. In a month's time, he was completely well. This bewildered Khilji. He was not able to believe that someone could cure someone without medicine. He felt extremely jealous of Bidyasagar. The treatment which the best of his hakims could not do in years, Bidyasagar did in a month. He termed their knowledge as a threat to him and his clan. *They are a threat to our rule. Their knowledge has to be destroyed.* He felt their knowledge was superior to his civilization. This gave him the feeling that they were an advanced race.

He decided the next day that he would destroy the greatest centre of learning. He attacked Nalanda monastery with his army. Every person caught was killed. Everything was set on fire. It is said the library of the Nalanda burnt for months. That day when Khilji attacked, Bidyasagar was in his room. When he came to know about it, he went looking for Smriti. He knew she would be killed if he didn't save her. He found her running towards the exit with Suryakanth. She stumbled into him and asked him to come with them. There was space for only two people in the little cart. It was already stuffed with people. Everybody was in a panicked state. He let Suryakanth and Smriti go. He would have gone had there been have been space, but his fate was against him. He saw Smriti fading in the horizon. He cried, he didn't know what had made Khilji attack the monastery. He was caught by the General of the Army and taken to Khilji who said, "This place should be destroyed. You made me feel you are better than us. This place has to disappear in the mouth of flames."

He now knew the reason was jealousy accompanied with sheer ignorance. He could not believe it could do such harm to humanity. He saw the ignorant soldiers cooking their evening meal by burning those great books. He could see what ignorance of a man could do. The general was ordered to kill Bidyasagar.

He took him in the far jungle. Bidyasagar seemed fearless from death. The general said, "I have a son, he has been sick since childhood. I took him to the best of hakims but he could not be cured. I know you can do wonders. I know you can cure him. I will let you go, just tell me the cure." Bidyasagar helped him out.

The general said, "You are dead to the world. Find some place in the forest and stay there for your whole life. You cannot treat anyone otherwise your news would reach the ears of Khilji and both of us would be killed. I am risking my life for you; I just want you to stay away from the eyes of the world. Bidyasagar has died. Understood? He is dead!" Bidyasagar nodded. He was released and walked deep into the forest and continued walking for a month. He reached the south of Magadha which was covered with a dense forest. He made a little hut there and began living a life of anonymity. The news soon spread that Bidyasagar was killed by Khilji who had now taken control of the area. The monastery burned for days and weeks after. Bidyasagar wept at what had happened; he should have told Bakhtiyar Khilji how he had treated him. As a consequence, he was now away from all his loved ones with a lonely life ahead.

He cried for the people who had died in the monastery. He cursed himself for the plight of Nalanda. He could still see those ignorant soldiers cooking their meal over burning books. It might have taken ages to write these books but they were lost in a moment's time. Everything was burnt to ashes. It takes years to create something beautiful but just a minute of flame to lose that piece of beauty.

He started farming near his hut, an art he learnt from Vikram's father. Every morning he would go for a walk into the dense forest. He would listen to the conversations of insects, animals and other forms of life. One morning he stopped near a tree which had a beehive. He listened to the bees talking amongst themselves.

"Every month a human comes and takes away our honey. They remain very happy with us because we have been turned into their slaves. We no more produce honey for our species because everything is taken by them. The best thing about humans is how they inflict cruelty with a smile. They would come with bags of smoke which they release upon us. We have to leave the beehive to save our lives. Many bees die in the act but they just want to own our honey, not our suffering. Human beings are lovers of slavery. They want every insect to be a honey-bee which could benefit their existence.

"They want every bird to be a hen, every animal to be a goat or a buffalo. They just want slaves for them. They could not face a free, wild spirit. They are against everything which is wild. They hate wilderness; this was the reason they left the jungles and settled in well-built villages and cities. They lost their wild spirit to selfishness and greed. Humans don't enjoy the chirping of a bird. They enjoy when a bird turns into a hen. They are lovers of hen, not wild crows."

Bidyasagar realized how right they were. *We have lost our wild spirit. We love slavery of all kind and we love slaves even more. First humans bought greed with their freedom. Now they want every wild being to be a tamed parrot. The people who live in the jungles and follow their wild instinct are called uncivilized. The creation of human civilization was against the foundation bricks of freedom. Man domesticated themselves and when they began a liking for domesticating. They moved to other animals. We could still be living in the jungle, freely like the wild animals.*

He walked back to listen to the conversation of the wild bees. He thought he had to uncivilize himself. He began living on fruits and berries of the jungle. He would float in the river like turtles. He was burning the domesticated creature within. He really felt he had been domesticated for years and the result was he too had become a slave of the civilization. He wanted to attain freedom from self. He would roam in the jungle the entire day and night, hearing the thoughts of wilderness. He could feel the river talking to him; its liquid tongue speaks greatly of the freedom. He was enjoying the wilderness. He began understanding why yetis chose to live away from the humans.

Bidyasagar would write poems on nature, he was turning himself into a wild spirit. He began abhorring human society and human civilization. He does not need a society to be happy. He just needs his wild spirit. Another morning while he was walking through the jungle he heard a cuckoo bird speaking of a human village where they caught a leopard and killed it.

"The leopard for them was a symbol of wilderness and they are against it. They love to be enslaved by the negative emotion and enslave other. Why do you think humans created cage? They want to enslave everything. They would enslave even their kind." The cuckoo predicted one day man would enslave their fellow beings in the name of civilization. It predicted slavery would be introduced within the realms of humanity.

The rivers said to him, "I fear my freedom will be annexed by the humans one day. I would be put to slavery where they would decide my course of flow. I saw a bad dream that I have been enslaved in some kind of embankment. I feel something is going to happen to me. We don't want to be civilized. I don't want to lose my freedom."

Bidyasagar consoled the crying river, "You will remain a wild river forever."

The river said, "Hope so."

One day a frog was speaking of the great riot taking place in a nearby city where hundreds of humans lost their lives. Hundreds of houses were burnt down. Bidyasagar was sadly listening to the news. The frog further said, "I saw a very ugly sight and I left the hole in that city. I liked living there initially but with time learnt jungle was a lot better place to be. Humans have lost their humaneness. They are the cruelest beast existing who claims themselves to be civilized creature but all they love is fire and flames."

Bidyasagar started enjoying his solitude. He would farm near his hut but mostly depended on the fruits and berries of the jungle. There was a squirrel who would come every day to his gate and would stare at him. For a week the squirrel kept coming to the hut. One day, the squirrel said, "Why is a man of city is living among us? He must be a spy from the human world." That squirrel doubted Bidyasagar.

Bidyasagar just smiled. The squirrel said to another squirrel, "Never trust a human. They would put you in cages." He wanted that squirrel to know not every human is same. He made a trap for the squirrel; he thought he would catch and then free it. The trap worked; the squirrel got caught. He could hear the squirrel crying for help and freed it the next moment. The squirrel was unable to understand why a man would free a creature from a trap.

The squirrel began to think why he freed it. He was capable of killing it then why did he catch it in the first place. The squirrel passed it on to every other squirrel that a man had attacked it, making a death trap for it. Every squirrel began fearing Bidyasagar. One day a storm came and the colony of the squirrel got destroyed. Bidysagar built a squirrel colony with his hard labour but the squirrels did not live in that colony again fearing the man would have done evil magic.

Bidyasagar was getting frustrated why the squirrels didn't believe him. He did everything. He then heard a voice from the jungle: *Don't try to prove that humans are kind; if they are there is no need to prove it.* He stopped after that. That same squirrel one day got caught in a snare. Bidyasagar saw and freed it. The squirrel announced in the colony that the man again put a snare for us. He smiled when he heard the accusation of the squirrels.

He left the hope they would ever consider humans as kind. Time passed and few days later, he saw a squirrel from the colony fall down from the branches of a tree. It was wounded badly so he brought it to his hut. For days he cared for it like his child. He never kept that squirrel in a close container. The squirrel began liking the company of Bidyasagar. It realized not all humans are bad. This time the squirrel went in the colony and announced that a man saved her life.

Bidyasagar realized why he shouldn't have tried to prove his kindness. The voice from the jungle has been right. If you truly are what you are trying to prove, the fact would come out one day or the other. Days passed and he began feeling lonely. He began feeling man is a social animal. He needs the company of others to be happy. One cannot live alone forever.

He walked to a nearby village and began living with people. For first few days he enjoyed their company but he could feel whatever he felt in the jungle to be true. *We have become slaves in the name of civilization and society. We are propagating our theory of slavery to all the beings.* He tried very hard to live there among the people but there was no peace. Every day the news came, Bakhtiyar Khilji has destroyed this village or some other village. He could see what a man could do with power. He could make power a slave to destroy the world. Bakhtiyar Khilji was destroying village after village with his mighty army. This is one face of our civilization. This is the civilization which we have built. The dictators and the tyrants rule the world and they destroy everything which is beautiful.

He thought all day if he was right in saving Khilji or had he made a terrible mistake. He was convinced it was his responsibility to save the life of a sick person and what could he do if that person turned out to be Khilji. He had no answers. He could not live for long in the society. There was something which always pushed him back to the forest. There was no doubt he was lonely in the forest. The nature gave him comfortable company but sometimes he felt the need of fellow beings. There was a happiness which nature brought out in him. There was a strange joy he felt amidst the woods. One evening he was walking towards the river and saw a beautiful moth dancing near the moon. The moth wanted to touch the moon but it had no idea how far the moon was. Sometimes the distance to paradise is so much that we choose hell to live. The paradise keeps moving farther and farther every moment, this is the tragedy of this race.

We are creating an artificial world where the walls of artificial covering would cover up the natural paintings of life. Bidyasagar found it very uncomfortable in the civilization of humans. He found jungle to be a lot more peaceful. Although life was hard but he remained lost in the stories of the jungles. One day when he returned from his evening walk, he found his hut on fire. He would never know who burnt it but it was obvious whoever had done so did not want him in the vicinity of the woods.

He built another hut nearby. He grew sadder and sadder. He saw a leopard axed down with iron axe. Life was suddenly not making any sense to him. He had harmed none still somebody burnt down his hut. There would be thousands and thousands such people whose houses were being burnt by an invisible monster. Every evening he writes few poems and burns it. He wants nobody to read his poetry. The poems are for no one but him.

It has become a ritual which was necessary for a good sleep. The poem which he burnt that day went like this:

I have seen the eyes of demon

And attended his evil sermon.

Don't let it attack,

The bear black.

Hide your soul behind the rabbit's burrow

So that you can run ahead of your shadow.

Goodness should always be praised.

Not a bird in this world should be caged.

It's evil, making of the cage.

Our mind is the devil's stage.

Don't let it play with your life's tale.

Burn the devil in the starry gases of hell.

Run away from the devil,

Become master of goodness, not devil's pupil.

Run, the devil is always near.

It lives in your fears

Like a parasite,

Like a termite.

It would make you hollow.

Like a python, it would love to swallow,

Your dreams, your world.

Make sure, your lips retain a smile

When you grow old.

Bidyasagar did not know anymore what he wants from life. He had witnessed the burning of the great Nalanda, he had seen people whom he loved die in the fire. He had seen himself in the past turn into a murderer out of greed of few coins. He was thinking of his long journey. The journey which began on the day he murdered the monk, who was a messenger of god. He wanted redemption from everything. He began to understand why Siddhartha left the worldly affairs: because it contained something evil. However hard you try to save the world from the fire, the flames seem determined to burn the world. Man is a fuel to that fire. He began writing again.

The illusions surrounding me,

Are rising high in the wind

Like flames,

Touched by it, my thoughts turn into ash.

Life is a wonderful gift but we turn it into a trash.

Wish I was that young child who could begin all fresh.

The news coming from the world of men is metals of stress

Which would hit my soul like arrows.

Life is a street of light in the labyrinth of shadows

But not all reach the light.

Some become creatures of night

And wander in the dark fields.

The ghosts come haunting whenever they close their eyelids.

I want to break free

From the clutches of an evil tree

Whose seeds have been sown by the society.

Free me, oh almighty.

I am tied with sins

Which has turned into grief.

There seem no relief

To my soul, my heart is aching.

The demon in me is taking

Everything from me.

We came together and built a society

But added flames to it,

Added evil games to it.

I am tired of playing,

Give me rest,

Give me peace.

He burnt the paper in flames and slept. In the morning the jungle was quiet. He woke up and left for a little walk. He felt lonely like that bat that he saw yesterday, flying alone in the black sky. He could feel the arrival of a cruel storm.

Upon his return he found his hut again on fire. Now he needed to know who had done this. There must be someone. Wind cannot do so without the assistance of someone. He wanted to find the person who was burning his hut as it was certain this person did not like his presence. This person wanted him to leave the jungle but he had once gone to dwell in the society, felt miserable and came back to the jungle. Yet once again someone was forcing him to leave.

8
The Wizard

The burning of his hut continued. Whenever he rebuilt it, it was found on fire on his return. Bidyasagar was sure whoever it was observed him very closely. While returning from the woods one day, he heard ants talking about the return of a wizard. Bidyasagar thought it could be the wizard behind the burning of his huts. The question was why he would burn down his hut?

For days he tried finding the wizard but he could not locate him. One day when he was returning from the walk, he saw a pigeon turning into a man. It must be the wizard, he thought. He hid behind the bushes and saw the wizard burn his hut with magic.

Bidysagar said in a grave voice, "I can see you." The moment he heard his voice, the wizard turned into a pigeon and flew away.

The wizard now knew he has been seen by the man. He realized there was no point in hiding. He turned, walked up to Bidyasagar and asked, "What are you doing here? This is my forest. I don't want any human to be around. I am sick of men destroying my forest bit by bit; slowly they are expanding their reach. They are growing like a plague all over the place. You must return."

Bidyasagar replied with an ease, "It was you who was burning my place of residence, not I."

The wizard laughed and said, "It was for the safety of the forest."

"I have no history of causing any harm to the forest."

The wizard smiled. "History cannot be trusted, my friend. It does not mean you are not capable of harming the forest, after all, you are a man."

Bidyasagar asked, "Oh, why? What does a man do?"

"They destroy."

Bidyasagar got impatient and asked, "Destroy what?"

"Everything." Bidyasagar thought he sounded like the yeti. The wizard asked in haste, "Do you know a yeti?"

Bidyasagar understood the wizard was monitoring his thoughts and nodded. "I met one on the mountains. He is a friend of mine."

"You must be extraordinary that a yeti visited you. You can live in my forest as long as you want." Soon the wizard became a good friend of Bidyasagar.

The wizard said, "I know sometimes you feel lonely but, my friend, loneliness is our closest ally." The wizard began talking about his journey to Frasenberg. A world in the roots of banyan tree; there are all sorts of creatures in that land. There are ostrich which could fly high in the sky. The sparrows are as large as the vultures. There is a witch who rules Frasenberg.

"A friend of mine has been captivated by the witch. I am going to rescue him from the palace of the witch. Will you come? Then you can ask for a wish from me." Bidyasagar thought over it and agreed. They disappeared in the roots of the great banyan. In no time they reached Frasenberg. Everything was beautiful here. There were fields of flowers. It felt they were in some another universe. They began walking and came across a sparrow. It was really as big as the vultures. The sparrow wished the wizard and asked, "Where are you going?" The wizard said, "To the Witch's palace." The sparrow complained the witch has poisoned the rivers of Frasenberg. The tiny whales have died. In Frasenberg the whales are the size of a finger. The wizard and the witch were in love once. Both lived happily in Frasenberg but then something happened. The witch began domesticating the doubts. One day the snake of doubt bit her, since that day she lost trust in everybody and began considering the wizard as her enemy too. She captivated another wizard who was a friend of the wizard. The snake of doubt and suspicion is very poisonous. It can turn anyone insane. Doubts without facts are a dangerous thing. The snake of doubt poisoned the mind of the witch and she began using her powers for destroying Frasenberg. There is only one way, the witch could be treated. She has to trust somebody but the poison of doubt will not let it happen.

The wizard sent Bidyasagar to the witch's palace. She was astonished to find an outsider. He said, "I am Bidyasagar. I am a friend of yours. You don't remember; we met last year but you must have forgotten me." The wizard had told him everything about the witch. Her mood swings, her favourite stories and everything else which he must know. In a month's time Bidyasagar and the witch became good friends. The witch began trusting Bidyasagar but one day the secret was out. The witch had come to know from her spies the truth. She captivated him as well.

The wizard walked in with flowers of trust. He planted flowers of trust in the garden of heart of the witch. The flower began blossoming. The poison of doubt began evaporating from her blood. She came into senses after a day. She freed Bidyasagar and thanked him for risking his life. She began telling her story. "The snake of doubt was without poison in the beginning. My mind added poison to the snake of doubts and made it poisonous. It began hissing, and then bit me. I began doubting everything, even the great wizard. My suspicion regarding everyone grew so much that I began to live alone. The curse of doubts and suspicion, it makes you lonely like hell." The wizard too thanked him as his friend was released by the witch and asked him to ask for the wish.

Bidyasagar said, "Tell me where Smriti is."

The wizard took few minutes and said, "She is living alone in the hills of Lavasha. She is sad and waiting for you." Bidyasagar now knew where she was and without another delay left for the hills. There she was living in one of the villages, a lonely life.

She lived in a small house and could not believe Bidyasagar was alive. Both began living happily. They would go to a lake every evening and sit down in the shadow of a tree. They would catch the setting sun together. This was a new beginning for Bidyasagar. After years of wandering and hardships, he was receiving the most beautiful gift of life yet again: love.

Their love began growing like a seed and soon turned into a great tree where birds of peace began chirping. The happy wings of the bird of peace began fluttering in harmony. It appeared life was a bird and they together constituted both wings of that harmonious bird. She would read out his poems sitting under a tree. He liked her recitation of his poems. She could see in afternoons he got restless. Smriti was living a very peaceful life with Bidyasagar. They would feed birds in spare time. He loved her laugh. This was a dream for him. This was the life he'd always wished for. He thanked the wizard every day for making him meet Smriti.

One afternoon his neighbour in the village fell ill. No one was able to treat her. Bidyasagar remembered he was advised by the general not to practice medicine at all. It could be dangerous but she would die if he would not treat her. After thinking for hours he decided to treat her, and saved her life. The news spread in the vicinity of the village. People began visiting him as the world is full of suffering and pain. People began visiting him with their illness. He would treat them taking nothing in return. Soon people from far began coming to visit him.

One day a young man came to him. He said, "I am tired of life. It is full of struggle. I don't wish to live more. I am tired of these struggles." Bidyasagar asked him to learn football. He began playing football every day. Bidyasagar made it a habit for him to play every evening. On evenings he could not find any one to play with. He became sad. Every day he would come to play but nobody will join him.

Finally, one day Bidyasagar called that young man and asked why he was sad.

"I could not find anyone to play with me."

"That's because I have asked them not to."

"But why?" he asked, shocked.

"Remember, one day you came to me complaining life is full of struggles? These players represent the elements of struggle in the game of life. Life would lose its meaning without them. Can you enjoy the game of football alone?" The young man shook his head.

"As I said, these players are like elements of struggle. They make life livable." The young man understood the message. Life has no meaning without struggle. We all have to struggle in life. We all have to play the game of life to feel the joy hidden in it. The young man no more complained of the struggle, he knew these struggles are like the players in football. They would challenge him but if he has to win the game, he has to keep playing. There would be friends and allies who would help him put the ball through the goalpost. These are players of his team but the game cannot be played without an opposite team who would try to defeat him. The opposite team is embodiment of struggle in itself.

Smriti was living a satisfied life. She would offer food to people who would come for treatment. Their services would make them known in the entire area. Soon the news reached Khilji. He sent his spy to know about this man who treated people free of cost. The spy came with news: this guy was Bidyasagar.

Bakhtiyar Khilji called his general and asked, "Did you kill Bidyasagar?"

The general confidently said, "Yes, I killed him." But he realized Khilji knew the truth so he admitted he hadn't. Khilji killed the general instantly and sent his best soldiers to kill Bidyasagar and his wife.

The soldiers reached their house. It was only Smriti in the there. The soldiers killed her and began looking for Bidyasagar. He could not be found. Bidyasagar had heard Smriti being murdered and was hiding in a corner and sobbing. His life with Smriti had just begun and everything was already over. His love had been killed by the soldiers of Bakhtiyar Khilji. Although the fate had yet again saved him, he was not able to understand why.

The next day, he again fled deep into the jungle as the soldiers were still looking for him everywhere. He met the wizard and asked, "Did you know this was going to happen?"

The wizard solemnly said, "Yes, I knew." Bidyasagar further asked why he didn't tell him. "I am not authorized to do that. If I would have told you, you wouldn't have spent those beautiful moments with her. Everything comes to end, be it love or life."

Bidyasagar made his hut again in the forest and began living a secret life, away from the hold of human civilization. In the morning when he woke up from his sleep, he found a strange sadness had walked into his heart. He could feel the cruelty of life. He complained the fate has not been kind to him.

He sat one evening at the river front. He could see the flying egrets nearby. He walked till the vicinity of a village where he could see people working in the paddy field. It was beautiful, the rain, the egrets. Smriti walked inside his landscape of memory. Few days back he was with her, smiling and playing in the monsoon rain. Today he was alone. He wanted to take revenge for her death. He felt he had saved the person and in turn killed her Smriti. He wanted to kill Bakhtiyar Khilji. He began thinking of a plan.

One day when he was roaming in the jungle, he heard a story from a frog. "Long back in the dark woods lived a cruel snake. The snake got a deadly disease. There in the nearby pond lived a community of frogs who knew the cure. The snake approached them and began praying on its invisible knees. The frogs saved the snake's life. Once its life was saved, he began killing the members of that frog community to satisfy its hunger. This was a clear betrayal. Time passed and the snake again became ill. He needed the medicine from the frogs but he had betrayed their community. The snake walked into the skin of another snake. He reached the vicinity of the pond and asked for the cure. The frogs told him the cure. Once the snake was cured, as usual he was going again to attack the frogs. But before he could reach the pond, a hawk attacked it and flew away with it between its sharp claws. The frogs later came to know that the snake they saved was the same snake but the fate took its course. The law of Karma is always working."

Bidyasagar began thinking karma would take its course. He began meditating more. He dropped the idea of taking revenge; rather he left the fate of Bakhtiyar Khilji on his karma.

The jungle grew more peaceful, he would see the peacocks dancing. His sadness took the shape of a wild elephant which wandered all the time in the forest of sorrow. That wild elephant wanted to escape the forest of fate where everything was uncertain. He roamed all through the forest like a monk. In the evening he would sit on a wooden chair and write.

A lonely crow sat on a branch,

And began looking at the forest floor.

There was a centipede,

Making round attempts to

Escape the eyes of passing wild cats.

Life is dear to all

But I often think what makes life a dear ground,

Maybe the seeds of the silent dreams.

The distant dreamy sky

Dazzles in each of our black eyes.

Without dreams, life is a barren field in the middle of desert.

Because in reality life is a desert,

A desert where the sands of sorrow has been spread to miles

And the terrain is burning in the fire of sadness.

It's only the rain of dry dreams

Which blow little life in each of us.

Maybe that centipede has a dream to reach the river of joy

And dance a little with the golden butterflies.

We all have such wild dreams.

Who are these wild cats,

Our enemies,

The enemies of life are no one

But own shadow falling bluntly on the river front.

The enemies are desires of caging the moon

In a cage of dust.

Our rust—the past keeps eating the soul,

The past has a carnivore spirit

Dissolved in it.

Then he did what he loved doing, he set those writings on fire. The fire inside him was burning everything outside. He was tired. One day he attended a sermon where a great eagle was speaking to all the birds. The eagle began, "Life is a dense labyrinth of desire. We all get lost in the way. I have seen birds dying in cages, lonely. It is the worst thing which could happen to a bird."The eagle was talking about the power of compassion. It had been once a cruel hunter and killed every little bird but one day it was sitting on a branch. An arrow was aimed towards it and just a moment before a little sparrow came and alerted it. The eagle said, "I was saved that day. I asked the sparrow why it saved me when I kill its kind. The sparrow said, 'Because I feel you would save sparrows one day.' I asked, 'Why would I do so?' It said, 'I know it because I could see an eye of eagle wet with tears.'" The eagle recalled the last day he killed a sparrow. He spoke about the killing to which the sparrow said, 'That sparrow was my father.' The eagle said in astonishment, 'You knew I killed your father?' The sparrow said in a grave tone, 'I knew that, still I saved your life because I know you have little kids out there in your nest waiting for you. I know how it feels to lose our loved ones. I didn't want your chicks to go through the same phase.'

The eagle promised that sparrow he would never kill a small bird but would rather protect them from other great birds. The eagle became the savior of little birds. It saved hundreds of life. Bidyasagar could relate to the eagle. His life had gone through this massive transformation too. He became a hermit who lived in the forest. He meditated and meditated hard. He could recall the rare joy of meditation which Vishwas has taught him. He could see human life is full of sorrow. He wanted redemption from sorrow. He wanted to be happy but the memories of Smriti always brought tears to his eyes. He must come out of the cocoon of grief, its meaningless, and the tears. How long one can be in sorrow? We should be like the leaves of lotuses, although submerged in the water but detached from the wetness.

Time passed. He was happy in himself. Every day he would hear stories from the creatures of the jungle. The creatures will talk of the human world, the stories of their cruelty. There was yet another riot taking place far away in some city, several pigeon's nest burnt away in that riot. The people flamed the houses of a man where these pigeons lived. The pigeons said the riot took place in the name of religion. They could not understand what kind of religion teaches burning down the houses. It's cruel. The pigeon told in detail the tales of horror. Bidyasagar pitied the humans. Whenever he remembered Bakhtiyar Khilji, he realized such were men.

He wanted to turn into anything but a man. The other day the pigeons told the story of a child who became an orphan in a night. Those groups of pigeons decided to come to the jungle and live. It was very risky to live near the vicinity of human world; there could be fire any time. Every day or the other Bidyasagar heard such gory stories.

He was fed up of humans and their way of life. There is too much greed, too much of wars, too much cruelty involved in their lives. He could see how peaceful the forest was. There was a perfect harmony here. He realized he should not mourn Smriti anymore, she is gone and that was the truth; remembering her would only bring tears. He wanted to free himself from the past. First the princess was gone, then Smriti. He understood he has repented enough. The karma took his course and took away everyone whom he loved.

Man is too obsessed with things. They think of nothing but material things. They have turned their life into a perfect mess. Bidyasagar could see all the vices of men. He could feel suffocation inside the body. He wanted to begin a new life but past always comes in the way as a hurdle. The past stays there in the life as a spirit which keeps haunting the life of every human. The other creatures like the birds and the trees are detached with their past. The human life revolves around shadows and material life. There is too much of wants of a human. A man cannot be satisfied with anything. He could feel the meaninglessness of human life. The yeti was right; men would destroy this world with their greed. Man has turned into a cruel breed. In the evening he took a paper and began writing.

"I have seen it; the sight of burning of the great Nalanda, a place of learning but ignorance of a man consumed everything. There is too much of ignorance in humankind. Man has a gift to reason but he has chosen ignorance as a way of life. Nalanda was such a great place, a place where a man could turn into Buddha from Siddhartha. The ignorance of human mind would destroy everything which is different from the imagination from self. His hatred for human life was growing but there seemed no way to get free. Thousands of Siddhartha could have enlightened and turned into Buddha through great books, the books which were lost forever. How many times man would have done such a blunder? They do it just out of their ignorance."

He pitied the ignorance of Bakhtiyar Khilji. The more he thought about the past, the more irritated he got with his present. He did not want his writing to reach the human realm of affairs. That day he burnt everything he had written about the past but he realized he was making the same mistake as Bakhtiyar Khilji. He was burning his writings out of ignorance. He could feel the presence of an ignorant being in himself. He decided he would conserve every piece from now on. There was no difference between him and Bakhtiyar Khilji. He decided he would write his poems and send them to Vikram. These writings may change someone's life for good.

He began thinking about Vikram that day, how he wanted to come to Nalanda and learn about philosophy, but now he could never do so. He has been ignorant. Although he did not want to be a man but he was still human. He decided he would leave behind the human image and turn into a yeti. He wanted to meet the yeti. He would ask the yeti to turn him into one of his beings. He no more wanted to be a human. He would leave the jungle and walk towards the high mountains after a year. He would prepare his mind to leave the human space and dwell in the wilderness forever.

He decided he would meditate hard and know the truth of nothingness. He agreed life was meaningless but there has to be something worth knowing by being a human. He decided he would learn the best virtues and would turn into a yeti. The idea of turning into a yeti fascinated him. It would be great if the yetis turned him into one of them through their magical power.

I would roam the wilderness as a snow leopard. I would never see the face of any ignorant being.

He realized the strength of an idea. The sun began to set; he decided to go for a walk.

9

The Wait

In a year he would leave the forest. He knows by now how much damage ignorance could induce in the heart of civilization. He wanted to kill the ignorance within his heart. Ignorance remains within us in the form of seeds of minute invisible parasite which suck upon our ability to deliver the best. Bidyasagar knew the only way to kill ignorance is by embracing the learning of nature. He began wandering more and more in the forts of nature. He would hear carefully more conversations among the creatures of the jungle.

He heard a turtle speaking to a community of fishes sitting on a rock. He was fascinated by the talk. The turtle spoke about the end of pessimism.

It said, "There is not a single pessimist being in this world. Every living soul is optimist because the lack of optimistic thought will make us kill ourselves. The mere existence of us in this world symbolizes the presence of optimism. Somewhere in our deep structure we always remain hopeful towards life. It is only the minute we completely feel hopeless, suicides takes place.

We all came across this fundamental question in our lives that what is this whole world about. We satisfy our thirst of this question by peeping through several philosophies. Finally, we choose one of the philosophies which satisfy our need. We all are postponing death every moment as we see a way where we can walk and escape death but mere escaping death is not enough, we should have answer with ourselves for our existence. There can be thousands of ways ahead of us but for survival, a person should have at least one way ahead of himself for walking. It's the minimum requirement for a living being. We may acquire pessimistic cover on ourselves but the core remains optimistic in nature. The experience is fundamental in shaping the outer covering but the inner core remains unaffected of the ongoing changes in human life. It does not mutate with drifting of the condition in life.

What makes us optimistic?

The uncertainties around death make us optimistic about this life as death represents the disappearance of the very way which is essential for our survival. Humans for centuries have struggled to find the world after death. Death is the point of no return and the way tends to disappear in the darkness which induces a fearful feeling in ourselves, which forces us to find a way. As the way always exists, it's only how hard we can think it makes it visible. It's the inability to think and find that invisible way which becomes the reason for suicide. The uncertainty pushes us towards the edge where we finally come with that much needed way for our survival."

He heard a green parrot speaking to a bee who was talking about a dream. It was moments just after the rain and the sky was still blended in a little blackness. The bee could see a river flowing far away. It knew the world was extremely beautiful before the arrival of humans. There was beauty dazzling and dancing everywhere, then man arrived with an ugly suitcase of self-illusion. The lie was spread that let man rule the world and it would be the most beautiful thing to ever have happened. Nature let man rule the world and he turned this it into an ugly place. The iron civilization of man lacked pigeon feathers in it. The tears of the great whales got diluted in the salinity of the sea. Bidyasagar was being convinced more and more that man could be the best creation for himself but for the rest he is the most barbaric breed ever produced from the womb of mother earth. The cruelty is, man does everything in the name of his great civilization. The dictator of hell must have been a human because man possesses the gift of being the most malevolent dictator. It's not a coincidence, birth of so many dictators; man loves to be a dictator. Human beings are just functioning as the dictators on the face of earth. They want the earth to function according to the wishes of man.

Bidyasagar thought the bee was right. Men are born like lotuses but soon they become Venus fly traps. This transformation of a lotus mind into a mind of Venus fly trap is the ugliest transformation.

The parrot disrupted, "Enough celebration of human vices but have you not heard of Buddha?"

The bee took its time. "Yes, we have stories which say he was in the favour of love for every breathing soul despite of its caricature."

The parrot said, "I agree. Man could be the cruelest of all but on the other hand it is only the man who can be kindest of all."

The bee interrupted, "Being kind does not justify being cruel."

Bidyasagar was quietly listening to the conversation.

There are so many good conversations taking place in nature. Nature has given voice to everything, even a river; the wind has a voice to them. He was fascinated upon hearing these voices. He wanted to hear it more and more. Few moments later there was a lovely conversation between the flowing river and a swan.

The swan asked the river, "Tell me something about you."

The river said, "I am not mere water but a dreamer. I dream of strange lands. I dream of beautiful valleys through which I flow; these valleys are where a river finds true happiness. I carry souls of millions in my flow. It is such a beautiful thing to walk on my liquid feet on the rocky terrains and the valleys."

The swan further asked, "Whom do you love the most?"

"The desert; it values me like no one else. I love the boatmen passing by, they speak of the human stories, and sometimes I feel life is a wonderful gift."

Next morning, he walked towards a lake in the middle of the forest. Bidyasagar sat on the shore. The sun was shining and rainbow appeared far up in the sky. The seven colors were the reflection of seven virtues embedded in human self. There were two hills romancing with each other. The gentle wind was rubbing his face softly. The invisible fingers of the wind wanted to wipe away the tears. Life appeared beautiful at the moment. He could see an old lighthouse on the other side of the lake. He felt so complete in himself like never before. That feeling of solitude was beautiful, just like the rainbow. The waves were gently hitting the shore, the lake wanted to expand its territory but the water was enslaved by the rocks. The enclosed water was dancing in circles for freedom. He could see restlessness in the water, the lake really wanted to expand like the universe but it could not free itself from the slavery of shores. The shapelessness of the sun's reflection was appearing like a face of a burning lantern. Something physical had restricted the expansion of the mysterious soul of the lake. The lake suddenly began speaking to Bidyasagar, "Man, come to me, feel the waves, the wind, everything wants to carry away your burden of guilt. Loose the burden and get free." The forest around the lake were green like dunes of heaven, the water of lake wanted to spread to another miles, dissolving distance in its liquid eyes. Wetness could be felt even without touching the water. The lake laughed like a happy camel, the birds chirping songs which were closer to their hearts. It was the freedom Bidyasagar wanted, freedom from the hold of human civilization. The jungle had mesmerized him with its wit and charm.

Bidyasagar spotted a fisherman catching fishes with his little net. He was silently moving with the waves like a wooden swan. Bidyasagar felt we all are fishes caught in the net. Those fishes wanted to jump back in the water. They were struggling to gulp air bubbles from their little gills. This inability of the poor fishes was creating a frustration in their heart, which would consume the radiating hope. He watched them die. Most of us die in a similar fashion.

Man is brilliant without his civilization. He could see another civilization in the interiors of the jungle, the nature had a civilization. He felt closer to it than the human one. Diversity was the key here. Suddenly the yeti came to his mind. He realized yeti was right; man should not have abandoned forest. He would have been really happy living with nature without adulteration. The greed whispered an evil dream into his ears and man got hypnotized by its charm. Bidyasagar could feel how meaningless life is without nature.

The fishing net of that distant fisherman was full of struggling fishes now. Although, few did manage to escape, these fishes will always know what it means to be free. Bidyasagar wanted to be one of those free fishes. He was trapped in the net and there, above in the kingdom of stars, there was a fisherman. He could see how restlessly those fishes in the net were struggling. Struggle against everything, struggle against the universe for freedom which every being needs to reach his potential. He heard two fishes talking in the lake. They were discussing an ancient tale which is close to the heart of every fish. "In the beginning everything was water. Everything was submerged in the vastness of that great sea. Fishes ruled the world. They were the most bright and beautiful creatures in the sea. Some fishes would grow like a star and twinkle in the heart of the ocean. A mystique fish called Brahma began imagining a world where the most conscious beings were walking the length and breadth of the newly formed land. They say Brahma imagined a paradise on earth. He imagined a species kind as him but another fish Ravana took birth. He began sowing seeds of greed and other evils in Brahma's dream. Unknowingly, Brahma created land in the heart of the ocean. A consciousness began spreading in the life forms. They evolved until man was born, the supreme conscious being, but Ravana had found a place in Brahma's dream. The good got blended with evil. This is the reason we constitute of both—the dream of Brahma and evil seeds of Ravana." Bidyasagar liked the story of the creation of man. Human became the most conscious being but Ravana in human mind turns good into evil. The blending of the good and evil was so perfect in itself; you cannot separate the two from the human mind.

Every creature has a story of origin. The ugliest thing Bidyasagar found in the evolutionary process was the creation of cage. Man created the concept of cage and enslaved his mind.

The sun had begun to set. A light began dancing on the roof of the distant light house. Bidyasagar got fascinated. He walked towards the ancient lighthouse. When he got close he saw a flock of fireflies had come together to create the most natural lamp. It was the most beautiful source of light he has ever seen. He came closer and could see the zig-zag moving, radiating particles with two wings. From a distance it appeared as if someone had turned on a lamp on the lighthouse. It was a brilliant blending of nature and man together. The lighthouse represented humans and the fireflies were the nature. The lighthouse must have been built by someone in the past. They would make a firefly lamp out of the desperate need to kill the darkness. We all want to kill the darkness and light up the lighthouse within our soul but we have killed the fireflies that once twinkled within like the thousands of stars put together. Soon evening lost its existence and the night was born.

Bidyasagar had forgotten everything, even his princess and Smriti. He was in love with himself at that moment. This was what he was looking for, since years. He fell in love with himself. Self-love was what he had been missing. There was no pleasure in it but a feeling of satisfaction. That's all he needed for the rest of his life. He wanted to love no one else except himself and nature. Nature was his true god, the god he had been looking for in the aisles of man.

Love yourself considering yourself a part of the nature. Man is not independent of nature irrespective how hard he tries to prove it.

He slept with these thoughts on his mind. In the morning when he woke up from his deep sleep. He has got his answer.

He decided he would leave the place in a week. Next day he went to pay homage to the banyan tree. This tree helped him pass his time. Numerous times he sat under this very tree and thought of life. We develop an attachment with a place, sometimes even a place where we have lived for a day. Bidyasagar had developed an attachment to the forest. It has been his place of residence for most of his life. He remembers a snail that he brought from a river. The snail complained, "I miss my homeland." But what is a homeland? It is not the place of birth but the place where we like living. He left the premises of human civilization ages ago. Every one discovers his homeland in his life time. The snail remembers the river where it crawled in the later phase of his life. It took him months to cover a kilometer of distance. Sometimes our homeland may coincide with motherland but home is a different experience. That snail's homeland was the river from where Bidyasagar had brought it to his hut. The snail complained of a strange boredom that thrives in human life.

Every day the snail would complain of being kidnapped from his homeland. He would tell stories of migrant snails who had to leave their homeland for finding tools of survival which is nothing but grass. Those snails never wanted to leave the place but sometimes in summer, the river begins to dry. Many have to leave to survive. They take with them a fragment of homeland in the shape of memory. Some return to their homeland after the rain, when river get flooded with water, but most do not. They settle down there but can there be only one homeland of any creature? The newly shifted place could be the new place of dwelling but they carry the memories and culture of their homeland. Mostly the homeland turns to be the place where we spend the best days of life, which is usually our childhood. The snail has never left the river even in the times of great crisis. Bidyasagar was fond of the snail. He found his theories of homeland interesting. Unlike the snail, it was in his adulthood he found his homeland. He was confused whether the high mountains are his homeland or it's the forest where he has lived most of his life. There was no doubt he had an affinity for forests but he loved the mountains the most. The snail was very clear in his thoughts that the river was his homeland but Bidyasagar was still struggling to find his. There is no doubt we all have a great affinity for the place of origin but it is not certain that the place of origin must be our homeland.

He decided to leave the snail back near the river. Bidyasagar has learnt from the snail the need of a homeland for every living being. We all are in search of our lost homes. We all are refugees in our own terms. The snail was extremely happy to know soon he would be in his homeland. That evening the snail told everything one should know to discover his homeland. "Few places make us feel like we have been here before. We feel so comfortable; it feels we have lived here in a past life." Bidyasagar was still in search of his homeland which he felt would be the mountains.

He really wanted the snail to be back in his homeland. We all miss our homeland even if we don't return to it. He wanted to ask the snail can't we have two homelands.

Bidyasagar said, "I feel I have two homelands. Why it is necessary to have only one homeland?"

The snail simply said, "I have only one homeland, the place where I grew up and saw the world changing." The snail had no answer to the question whether we can have multiple homeland or we have only single homeland in our lifetime. The snail knew he had only one homeland that was the river where he wanted to return and live the rest of his life in the wetness.

In the evening, Bidyasagar took the snail to the river and left him. He could see the joy in the snail's eyes upon returning to the river. The snail thanked him for making it learn the importance of homeland. It's only when it was taken from here he realized what a homeland is.

Bidyasagar walked back to his hut. He was to leave tomorrow for the mountains. He sat down and began writing.

"I am excited to go back to the high mountains. I feel it might be my homeland. It is here that I would find that rare joy the snail was talking about. Further, I would not like to return from there if it turns out to be true. I have changed a lot but I am tired of being a man. I want to shed the human skin and turn into something else. There is too much of misery in the world of men. Many of these are our own invention. We, as a collective civilization, have invented these miseries in our little head which would cease to exist if we ceased to exist as a civilization. I am tired looking at men being evil."

He would never forget the burning of Nalanda monastery. That incident would always remain in his memory. Although he does not miss Smriti anymore but he could feel there was a sense of fulfillment while living with her. That's the tragedy of our lives, we can't decide our lives. We could decide our fates but not our lives.

Next day, Bidyasagar began his long journey to the mountains. It would take weeks to reach those mountains. He was happy and excited. Like the last time, first he had to cross deep woods where few would walk. For men, these forests could be cursed but for him, forests are among the most beautiful places to dwell. It was said a yaksha lived here.

10
The Yaksha

After walking for three days, he reached a village. There were cattle walking on the dusty road. He was once again close to the heart of human civilization. He decided to rest in that village for the night. He was lying under the shade of a tree, looking at the beautiful space around him. The flowers of rajnigandha were blossoming at some distance. The village road was quiet. There were jackals howling behind the bushes.

He saw a cat crossing the silent street of the village. It looked at him suspiciously as he was an outsider. Soon came two grasshoppers and began jumping around. They were talking out loud and wondering if there could be as many Earths as there were humans, would people be happy then? Would then they be satisfied and happy? If each human had an earth to live on, would there be no wars? The other grasshopper said, "I don't think so. They would still find a reason to destroy each other's worlds. They would think of conquering all the planets inhabited by fellow beings. They would not be happily living in the planets they would be given. They would find means to conquer other planets. That's human nature, to conquer and expand."

Even if there were billions of earths with a single person on each, there would be no peace. There always would be few who would prefer war. Bidyasagar agreed with the other grasshopper. Man is fond of violence just as young are fond of love. Next morning he left. Soon the chirping of humans got lost in the surrounding. He saw a baby elephant fallen in a pit. It looked scared. He could see in its eyes the fear which he almost always saw in every animal's eyes when he used to catch them in the past. He could feel the suffering of that baby elephant. He thought we all are that little elephant fallen in the dark abyss. We are trapped and want to be free from the vicious fate. He could see the struggle of entire human race in the form of that elephant. Somewhere or the other there is struggle linked to our very existence. Soon he began to see himself in that elephant, he wanted to free that elephant from the pit. He began trying but suddenly was attacked by another elephant who appeared to be her mother. The mother took him to be the hunter. He had to decide either to save the baby elephant or himself from the fury of her mother. He decided to save the baby elephant at any cost but it was a risky affair. He could be killed by the mother who was angry and frustrated with the world for being so cruel. He was trying to save the fallen elephant but she was reluctant to believe him. It is very hard for these creatures to believe a human being. For them, humans are to be feared not trusted. He got a wooden climber, cut it down and made a little rope to rescue the elephant. He was attacked twice by the mother before disappearing, probably to call her herd. He had to save the fallen elephant before the arrival of its herd. He tried hard and finally was able to bring it out of the pit. Soon arrived its herd. He ran and saved his life. After walking a little appeared the yaksha laughing. The yaksha praised him for his courage.

It said in a grave tone, "I am Yaksha, the forest spirit.

This was my doing. You are a brave person. Tell me, where are you going?"

"I am going to the mountains."

The Yaksha said, "I have a question to ask, nobody has been able to give an appropriate answer till date." It pointed at a large spider, sticking on its web. "This is a hungry spider, he needs his next meal in an hour otherwise it would die." Soon a big butterfly came and got caught in the web. This was a strange situation; the spider was hungry and moving towards the butterfly. If he did nothing, the butterfly would be killed by the spider and if he saves the butterfly the spider would die of hunger. He had to save one but he was confused whom to save, the spider or the butterfly. He thought and decided to do nothing this time. He watched while the spider killed the butterfly and ate its flesh. The dead wings hung down the web.

The Yaksha asked, "Why did you let the butterfly die?"

"This is the course of nature and I should not come in between."

"Why did you save the baby elephant then? That too was a course of nature."

Bidyasagar shook his head. "There is a difference between both the situations. That was not a course of nature. Humans have created another self apart from his natural self. That trap was by a hunter to catch an adult elephant so that he could kill it for its tusk but unfortunately the baby elephant got trapped. Humans can live without the tusk; it's not his need but an artificial one created out of greed. In the latter case, the butterfly was the need of the spider, the basic need of life. It shouldn't be interfered with otherwise the spider would have died."

The Yaksha laughed, "The elephant being killed by the hunter is cruel but so is the killing of a butterfly but you are right, that butterfly was the basic need of life, man's basic need is no different from other creatures but he pretends that he needs it all to satisfy his ego."

Bidyasagar was getting annoyed. The Yaksha asked, "Do you not think humans are also a part of nature?"

"Of course, but nature made a mistake by creating the man. He is not an ordinary incarnation of life but a perfect amalgamation of mind and soul. Nature gifted a higher form of consciousness to human, this consciousness made them self-aware. They began creating another world using their consciousness."

"What do you want to say? The creation of human beings was a mistake by the nature?"

Bidyasagar replied, "Only time will tell. The way humans are progressing is a concern for nature."

The yaksha was impressed by Bidyasagar. He said, "In the future, humans are going to ruin the world with the gift of their consciousness. It is a prophecy but we all are governed by our karma. Man would also create an artificial aspect of himself which would ultimately destroy human form. As nature created humans, humans would create an antagonist nature from their consciousness."

Bidyasagar replied, "I didn't get you."

The Yaksha said, "Few hundred years from now Humans would create highest form of artificial intelligence which would be the artificial replication of human intelligence. He would create self-image in the form of artificial man."

Bidyasagar interrupted, "Who are these artificial men?"

"These artificial men would be human like intelligent machines. They would be gifted artificial intelligence in much the same way the way nature gifted humans an intelligence which they misused for their artificial growth. The artificial man would have their own civilization much like man does. They would destroy human civilization and create an empire for themselves; just the way man destroyed nature's civilization and created his own. The karma would unfold in a unique way and man would only create his destruction himself."

Bidyasagar was introduced to a new perspective. He was not happy to know how humans as a race would get destroyed. Man would create an artificial man. This was confusing for him. He realized there is no threat to humans except human mind itself. It was a fascinating story for Bidyasagar. He wanted to save humans from going astray and get lost in the kingdom of greed. The only way humans could possibly evade their destruction was by giving place to nature in the civilization. Humans have to remember karma is always at work. If humans would show generosity to nature then time would show generosity to them. Everything in this world is two ways. Nobody can save man but man himself.

Nature has to be protected if humans want to protect their civilization. Bidyasagar understood everything. The Yaksha asked Bidyasagar to stay with him for few days. He told the Yaksha about the yeti. The Yaksha said the yetis are the representative of nature's civilization. Humans have their own civilization. In future there would be a clash between these two great civilizations. The yetis would be fighting for natural world and man for the artificial world. There would be a collision.

Bidyasagar wanted to be on the side of nature when the conflict eventually takes place but not fight the war. He said, "Nature has created us, putting its faith in our intelligence. We can't let Mother Nature lose her motherhood. We have abandoned her because we want to be the new rulers."

It is strange the creator is being destroyed by its own creation. As the reach would expand, the destruction would progress. The Yaksha said, "One day humans would destroy the moon. They would end up drilling the planets which we know. The gift of humans would be an instrument of exploitation."

Further it said, "For nature, man and pigeon are equal but humans are against any kind of equality. I wonder what makes man think he deserves all that he can see. Humans have captured the land, even sea. They pretend to be the lord of the earth. They escape their responsibility sitting on the boat of superiority. Men cannot follow the equality rule because even mankind is cursed with the venom of inequality. They have created a hierarchical ladder where they segregate their own kind based on several discourse. A pigeon plays an equal role in maintaining order in the forest but it is not given its due. An earthworm works equally hard to sustain the fertility of the soil but all fruit is reaped by humans. They are inherently dictators. They dictate the terms of managing the earth. All living creatures are bonded universally. They have forgotten the rules of nature. There are many like crocodiles and lizards which have been here before us.

"There are fishes which have been swimming in the

vast ocean like kings but all living creatures have been reduced to slaves of humans. Every creature who is not slave of humans is in danger. Humans loved slavery from ancient times. Earthworms want to revolt against the cruel empire of men but men are shrewd creatures. They have created ideologies of compassion which is followed by none. Humans have no ideology which they could practice.

"Freedom is man's distant goal; they can't be free until they give freedom to the colonized nature. The colonization of nature began with cutting down first set of trees for weaving space in the dense canopy of forest. Nobody can be happy being a colony of any empire."

The Yaksha again mentioned of the law of karma. Artificial man would take control, wiping out the human race as the most dominant breed of the planet earth. Everything has to come to an end, this is universal law. Nature should be respected with all its due. Karma of mankind would decide the fate of mankind.

The rivers would go dry; the ponds would turn into a fissured land. The forests will be without wilderness. The sky would go bird less, the oceans would go fishless. This would be the end. The artificial man would not need nature for its existence. The nature would get lost forever in the void of darkness. The artificial man would be the new breed of machines which would colonize other heavenly bodies in outer space.

This would happen again, the creation will take control of the creator. This time artificial man would rule the world in same way as humans did. Bidyasagar realized the dangers which humans possessed to the natural world and the danger artificial man possessed to humans. He imagined a world without a bird's song. There would be no song but the song of the dead. He asked the yaksha how nature could be saved. He said, "Humans had to be made to understand the importance of nature and the law of karma."

It took Bidyasagar to an old temple where he showed how a spider was living in a statue. Gods of human are kind but man as a god is the cruelest being. It was a very old temple. Humans had abandoned the place and nature had returned.

Bidyasagar would stay for two more days and then leave for the mountains. The Yaksha said, "Listen carefully, there would be a conflict between humans and yetis few hundred years down the line. Humans would fight with their weapons and yetis would fight with their magical powers. Turn into a yeti and fight for nature's right because it is the right thing to do." Bidyasagar too was fed up of the human world, seeing enough of savagery to other forms of life Bidyasagar wanted humans to change so that they would avoid war.

He was ready mentally to turn into a yeti but the question was will yetis accept him in their secret clan of snow leopards? The Yaksha had shown him the great path. He was against the artificial civilization.

It said he would fight with the yetis against the humans. A war would happen that would engulf everything. "I don't know if we will win or lose but there has to be someone who would tell the humans about their wrong doings. I know there are few people who want to save nature. They have taken birth in the wrong species. They would have been a lot happier if they were in the clan of yetis instead. There is a section of people who want to live in the shade of nature.

Yetis and such men should unite against the expansion of the artificial civilization."

The most immediate question which often bothered him was whether the yetis would accept him as one of their own. The Yaksha said, "I have no ill will against humans but I am against their artificial civilization. I know you are a poet. I have seen you writing poetry in your spare time. Can you recite a few for me?"

Surprised and pleased, Bidyasagar pushed all other thoughts out of his head and started reciting poems for the Yaksha.

I have tasted it all.

The sweet rise and the bitter fall.

I have played enough roles,

Seen enough of potholes

On way to true god.

Blood in my hand,

Blood is in the sand.

Red is the water,

Red is the colour of desire.

Red is the flame and fire.

Don't get fooled by the liar.

Don't murder your good thoughts

Turning mind into General Dyer.

Don't massacre

The good thoughts of wisdom.

Run from this evil kingdom

Towards your real home.

Like everyone the Yaksha liked his poem and asked him to recite another. He began,

A butterfly is drowning in the pond of wind.

There is something at a distance, her eyes want to build.

With time, the bones of a butterfly get filled with mud and silt.

The flowers of happiness get ruined

In the rain and thunder

And we wonder.

Where are our glorious wings?

The rats of despair has gnawed the lovely rings

Of hope tattooed by the god on her wings.

She laughs over the loss,

Sitting with her legs crossed.

She didn't want to leave the fort of joy but she was forced

By the demons of heaven.

The Yaksha asked Bidyasagar to follow him. He showed him a hidden natural wonder. It explained there are many worlds within the world. These birds are relative of yetis. Yetis too have their secret world, unseen by the human eyes. There was a bird as large as an elephant which could spit fire.The Yaksha said there are only eleven such birds and yetis know about them. They live in the form of sparrows. They know if man came to know about them, they would be caged in no time. They hardly turn into their real form. Bidyasagar was really surprised to see that great bird. There were mammoth butterflies moving in their windy herd. They were talking about depression. In coming years, people would grow depressed. They would be restless, lonely without nature. The mammoth butterflies were now dancing like peacocks.

One morning while Bidyasagar was on a little tour of the jungle, he came across a black bear talking to a red panda. The black bear was speaking, "I was captivated by humans long back. I have seen their world from up close. They used to make me dance on the streets. I can survive any jungle because I have lived with men. Man is the strangest beast of all. He is the greatest paradox of nature. He could be the kindest and the cruelest at same time. The man who captivated me was a poor man. I would never understand their world. Humans have complex emotions, different from us. They could be laughing due to sadness and misery. We cry when we are in pain, they could shed tear in happiness."

The red panda yelled, "What? Can anyone laugh in extreme pain?"

The black bear said, "Yes, humans do so sometimes. They could kill all the birds for their fake happiness. The existence of binary of good and evil is not the problem; the problem is creation of unbalance between the binaries. The bad exceeds good in proportion but the human world does not cease to exist. The human society would be at its best when goodness will beat the ugliness of human self. The artificial man which man is creating would be devoid of the good and bad."

The red panda began yawning. "Sleep, bear, you have lost your mind. I am not going to listen anymore."

The black bear got angry. "It's the reality!" He yelled. "Our existence will be threatened by this species in future. They are the most expansionist breed."

The bear continued, "I noticed humans love to adore their creation. Once, the world was beautiful like the sky. I have seen men still feel good in the woods but he has walked light-years from his true home. I have seen humans to be truly happy in the lap of nature but then why did they leave their home? They leave what they love and go for the suffering. Humans have chosen their suffering thinking it to be redemption from the suffering." The bear was right. Every human is suffering in silence. They created the society out of the need for mutual cooperation for growth but human growth has been negative. They have grown inside the land of darkness like any seed. They need sunlight to come out of the land and turn into a plant of hope.

The bear said, "Humans have to return from the debris of dead rivers to a new shore. The sunken boats of nature have to reemerge from the bottom of the dark pit of rivers and show a new way to the people lost in the sea. The civilization of nature is shrinking every day with the great expansion of the artificial civilization."

The red panda was asleep by now. The bear was silent and after a while began looking at a group of owls flying away. The night was growing darker and darker. The bear could not understand why he hated the human world. There was something nasty about humans. They carry a strange sadness in their soul which is the result of walking away from the nature and towards the shore of artificial need.

The whole day Bidyasagar listened to the conversations between the two, now he too was tired. He began thinking greed is the natural ingredient of human feelings or we have grown it from the artificial modicums. But he believed greed to be the natural ingredient in the box of human emotion. He was confused. He wanted to reach the high mountains soon. He met the Yaksha and asked for permission to leave. The Yaksha wished him good luck for the journey. It said, "Humans have to realize the artificial civilization cannot exist without the gift of nature. It is imminent to save nature."

Bidyasagar began walking towards the high mountains. It would take days to reach there but he was excited to meet the yeti. He had thought of a name for the yeti, he would call him Himputra. He needed to find him. The biggest question was whether he would be allowed to turn into a yeti and leave the human skin. He was not sure of anything except one—he wanted to turn into a yeti. With these thoughts, he kept walking towards his destination. The land began getting elevated and the vegetation began changing with the changing latitudes.

11

Homeland

Soon he was surrounded by snow from all sides. He felt as if he had reached his homeland. He could understand what the snail felt on reaching the river which was its homeland. He felt more than anywhere else he belonged to those snowy peaks. He has finally found his homeland. He needed to meet the yeti. He went to the village where he had stayed the last time. The house was still empty. He found Vishwas playing in the snow, a grown-up version of him. Time has Midas's touch, only it turns you old instead of gold. Vishwas was very happy to find Bidyasagar back. They sat and talked of everything they could. At night while Vishwas slept, he walked out to look for the yeti. He could not see a shadow out in the snow.

He could see the heartbreaking beauty of the mountains. In the distance, he could see few lamps. Everyone was asleep. The lamp was the invention of man, but not fire. The linear progress of time is bent, moving in circles. He thought not all can walk back to the forest and live the natural life which was given to us. This life we have invented is much like we invented god. We need god for a time being only to abandon him later much like nature. The nature was once human's god but they turned god's empire into dust. He wanted to ask the yeti if it was possible for humans to walk back into the forest. Further, he thought the time when humans lived in the jungles were their childhood period. We all adore childhood. The mankind grew from its nascent stage to the present form. There existed many intermediary stages between the childhood and youth. Mankind is in its youth in the present time. Humans have done wonders with their mind. They can't go back to live in the jungle but they do miss their childhood, and that's why man still enjoys the solitude of the forests. We should respect nature as we have risen from it. A more intriguing thought visited Bidyasagar. He has been friends with a remote tribe. Something clicked in his mind. He understood what these forest men are — they are the children of mankind. They should be loved and respected for their childhood. As we rejoice looking at children playing in the field, we should rejoice looking these *forestmen*. They still live in the jungle and play in the green cradle. He really wanted to ask the yeti but he could not find him that night.

Next morning he walked back to the house. Vishwas woke up to find Bidyasagar sleeping. He slept the whole afternoon and left the bed in the evening. Vishwas said, "I think you were too tired." Bidyasagar just smiled. They walked out to the see the setting sun. The sinking sun was spreading its dying rays out over the snow. The yellowness got lost in the whiteness of the snow. Vishwas asked, "Are you back here to stay?" Bidyasagar replied, "Yes, these peaks will be my homeland from now." They talked then, sitting on a rock and later returned home. Bidyasagar decided to go to the peaks the next morning and stay for a week. He took ration on two yaks and started walking. He wanted to meet Vishwas before he left but he was getting late. Once there, he put his tent up, made of thick animal fur. It was freezing up there on the peak. He set up a fire and sat down with his palms out towards it, taking in as much heat as he could. The smoke was a signal of his arrival. He wanted desperately to meet the yeti but he could not be found anywhere. He had not spotted a single snow leopard since he arrived. Three days were gone already. He was getting more and more anxious now.

On the fourth day, he spotted a snow leopard. While he was elated for a moment, he wondered if it was the yeti or just a regular snow leopard. He remembered what the yeti had told him, that not every snow leopard is a yeti. He tried calling him. He shouted *yeti, yeti,* but the snow leopard had disappeared.

He thought that must not be a yeti. Two more days passed but there was no sign of it. One night when he was sleeping he found something moving. When he came out, it was the yeti. The yeti smiled looking at Bidyasagar.

"I knew one day you would return. I did not wait but I knew one day you would come here forever." Bidyasagar told him everything from the fall of the great Nalanda, his counter with Bhaktiyar Khilji and Smriti. He told him in detail how the ignorance of one man destroyed the greatest place of learning on the face of earth. The yeti listened to everything with interest.

He said, "Just imagine what the ignorance of the entire mankind would do. It could destroy everything which is beautiful."

Further Bidyasagar told him, "I have found a name for you. You will be called Himputra."

Later, Bidyasagar got lost in his thoughts. Himputra said, "I could give you magical powers; you could avenge the death of Smriti. I know the loss of loved ones is painful. I have also lost my grandfather to a yeti fight. Long back, there was a yeti named Dogga. He wanted to become the leader of the yetis. He began using his magical powers for evil purposes. He brainwashed the several yetis. He wanted to establish a Yeti rule in the world. He wanted them to leave the wilderness and begin a yeti society similar to humans. Dogga was very ambitious; according to him Yetis have spent enough time with nature. It is time to establish new world where Yetis would be the ruler, not humans. My grandfather, Jatayu, decided to oppose Dogga. Jatayu said, 'A yeti should not leave the wilderness. We are at the service of mother earth, we can't betray her.' My grandfather challenged him. Jatayu was killed but it united the yetis against Dogga. He was ostracized from our community and peace returned to the yeti world. I could help you kill Khilji."

Bidyasagar thought for a moment and said, "I don't want to kill him, rather I want to kill his ignorance. He is not the enemy but his ignorance is. He wouldn't have burnt down Nalanda if only he knew the treasure it was. The flames were rising high in the darkness of his mind and the ignorance fueled the fire." Bidyasagar paused for a minute and said, "You are right, we are too ignorant. Human ignorance should be killed. This ignorance is the most fermented vice of all. It would be foolish to kill Bakhtiyar Khilji. It would yield nothing. Death is momentary; soon another Khilji would take birth. The only way to preserve the world in its true form is to kill the human ignorance. We are too caught up by the ephemeral beauty of the human world. Man was the happiest creature in the past, now he is the saddest of all."

"The sadness would only grow, to an extent that it would consume the world. They will create a fake happiness which would be nothing but a mixture of greed and lust. Like their civilization, their happiness would also be artificial." Bidyasagar narrated the conversation he'd had with the Yaksha.

The yeti was listening carefully. He could see Bidyasagar has become a wiser person. He said, "Nalanda must be a great place." Bidyasagar said it was. "I also think humans would turn into an invasive species with time. They love nothing but to conquer."

Bidyasagar then said, "I want to turn into a yeti. I am tired of men."

The yeti was surprised. He said, "In order to become one, you have to make the abandoned nature your god once again."

Bidyasagar smiled. "Nature is the real god. The wild rivers are saints of nature. The mountains are stoics. The deer are hermits." He took a deep breath. "I have seen a man doing ugly things to a man which no one else would do. I am sick of humans who think nothing beyond the horizon of greed. The sun is lost from the horizons of their civilization. There is a perpetual darkness which is spreading at a terrible speed."

"You can turn into a yeti but it can only happen with the permission of the entire yeti community. That's a tough job to do."

Himputra promised to put the proposal of turning Bidyasagar into a yeti in front of the community. "You have to attend the secret meeting of yetis which takes place once in a year. Luckily that meeting is bound to take place this full moon." Bidyasagar was excited. He was ready to turn into a yeti. The tiredness of being a man was tremendous. He agreed to attend the meet with the yetis. Himputra said, "Let me tell you about the future, in the meantime. After hundreds of years, there would arrive ultra modern humans. They would create an improvised version of hell and will name it Heaven. They would magnify the human ignorance to a new level. The earth will turn into a garbage bag. Greed will be the new angel of men. Man would create new substance called plastic and everything would turn into plastic. Man would turn into a curse king, whatever he would touch would turn into plastic. Even his dreams would be made up of plastic. He would rob nature of its wilderness. There would be just humans on every shore and segment of the earth. Over population of humans would be the greatest menace for earth. They would enslave nature. The water would be polluted beyond a point that the fishes won't survive. The lions and the tigers would just be just another cat to him living in cages."

"There will be no wild river but only faint reminiscence of those rivers. His food, his mood everything would be artificial. I fear we have to fight a war with humans to protect the earth. Would you fight for Nature?"

Bidyasagar replied, "It is a complex question. I promised someone that I would never take part in a war."

Himputra said, "We don't have much of an option. If we won't fight, she would become a barren territory of dust. We can't let earth's beauty disappear. Hundreds of species would be going extinct every day. The planet would never see extinction at such massive scale again. These extinctions would be human induced. The worst part is, it could have been avoided but they have always surrendered to greed.

Nothing will be left on the face of earth which is not a part of human's artificial civilization. There would be no rainforest but desert. There would be no jaguar, no tiger, no rhino but man and his artificial empire. You want these kind birds to die without any fault? These mute creatures have done no crime but still are at the receiving end of it. The tortoise would be gone, the butterflies would be extinct. It is a terrible crime. Somebody has to fight the human greed, even if we know we would lose the war because man is the most powerful beast ever born on this planet." After listening to his concern, Bidyasagar gave his consent. Himputra said, "You will come to know our secret if you turn into a yeti; I can't tell you that now."

Bidyasagar asked again, "Humans cannot go back to their old home?"

The yeti replied, "They cannot. They have walked too far on their road. They should rather give space to nature in their world. But they refuse to do so. They don't want to be second to nature. Everything grows up, even humanity. The worst thing about men is they want to displace nature with their artificial self. They have walked too far on the wrong road and they cannot walk back. The road which you are talking about is lost forever. Humans have been moving in the wrong direction for ages now. They have built a new road for themselves, carving that road does not make them greater than nature." Bidyasagar could see the future appeared bleak. He wanted to see the change the humans would make. He wanted to witness everything. He felt he knew man because he has been one for his whole life.

Himputra added, "We should not forget from where we have come from? Humans should respect their past and should weave space for nature in future."

Bidyasagar wanted to meet Vishwas one last time. He told Himputra he would see him the day after as there was someone he wanted to meet first. He walked down to the village and found Vishwas reading a book. He told him he was leaving the next day.

"Where are you going? You said you would live in the mountains forever."

"Yes, I will, but away from the village. We will meet again and I'd be around."

Vishwas asked again where he was going and Bidyasagar repeated that he would be around. They spent the night talking. In the morning when Bidyasagar woke up, Vishwas was sleeping peacefully. He did not want to wake him up. He left for the peak. He called Himputra and he came half asleep. Tonight, he would be taken to the secret community of yetis.

Bidyasagar was excited to meet them. There would be thousands of yetis meeting tonight far away in those mountains where lives no man only snow leopards. Soon the sun went down he reached the peak where the meeting was organized. It was mid night; the full moon was shining like a diamond.

He reached at the spot with Himputra. There he saw thousands of snow leopards. When he arrived they turned into yetis. They were walking in the snow singing a song

Life is a journey to beautiful dreams.

Glaciers of happiness would turn into silent streams,

Flowing on the slippery rocks of grief.

Don't rob the forest of its bird song turning into a thief.

We would dance and tap our feet.

Wait for us, oh man, we would come to meet.

We are worried because you have forgotten

This life is gift and the earth is Eden.

He was hypnotized by the sight. He had never seen such thing.

Himputra announced, "This is the man I was talking about. He wants to be one of us. He wants to save mother earth from being destroyed. I have lived a long time in the forest and known all the creatures through their conversations. Every creature has a concern regarding the growing interference of man, in all aspects of life." Himputra turned to Bidyasagar."You were accepted the day you said you did not want to avenge Bakhtiyar Khilji but only kill his ignorance. You have the qualities we yetis have. You are courageous, peace loving, most of all, you are thinker and a poet like us. You appreciate the beauty of mother earth." There was a ceremony where every yeti sacrificed few drops of blood. Himputra collected those blood drops and offered to the fire god. The yeti blood was burnt in the fire and the fumes which rose turned Bidyasagar into a yeti. Yetis were dancing around him. They began speaking some magical words in their language. Himputra was the leader of the yetis. This did not surprise him as he could see Himputra was the best thinker he has ever met. Himputra said, "We don't expand our material needs. We have our social organization. The leader is elected on the basis of their thoughts. The thinkers and philosophers turn into our leaders. You humans are turning into a homogeneous breed, there is a growing uniformity in thoughts, ideas and way of living. You have left thinking behind and found other interests in life. We can see the more material civilization is growing; more you are losing out on thinking about the fundamentals of life. Philosophers should have been the kings. There is too much we could learn from nature. You must know the yeti gods. You should take the blessings of the yeti gods. These gods are no one but the nature itself. The most powerful of yeti gods are jaguars. Water and fire are most pious gods, we value water and fire more than anything, although they are opposite in nature but essential for life. We have crow god too. There are hundreds of yeti gods and you should take their blessings. We worship nature in its all forms."

Himputra said, "Welcome to the yeti tribe." He could not believe it. He was told the greatest secrets of yetis. "We are everywhere not just in these mountains protecting nature. We can take the form of bees and alligators. The truth is, we could take any form of life which has ever existed on the face of the earth. We could turn into any living being of our choice. This is the greatest gift yetis have been given, anything but human. Any Yeti, who turns into a human, even once, would be ostracized from the yeti world. You have to give your word you would never turn into a human again. Nature has created its greatest form in the form of yetis. We are the inheritors of nature's legacy. We would give every chance to man to change their path. We would wait for hundreds of years. We would wait and see if man could change and love nature again in its true form."

Bidyasagar was now a yeti. Himputra asked, "Which form do you wish to take?"

"A snow leopard like you," he said and began reciting a poem.

Snow Leopard

Here, there are no footprints of smoke
In these snow-covered rocks.
Standing alone on the edges of these steep slopes
Reunites my heart with lost hope.

The wind here is thinner than paper
But it does not flatter,
The eternal silence stops the continuous chatter
Of the mind,
It is this place where one finds
Life is tough, it's not kind.

This white solitude is my nest
Where I dwell and rest.
Here exists no one other than me
Not a beast or a bird.
I am the king of these high mountains,
I am a snow leopard.

He was surprised to know yetis could take any form. Mostly they pass their time in the form of animals living in extreme temperatures as there are fewer men in these harsh climates. They want to live a peaceful life, away from the human civilization. Many have taken the form of blue whales and swim in the sea. Many roam as bees living in the Siberian wilderness. Bidyasagar tried turning into a bee and in no time he was buzzing in the snow. He found the climate was too cold for a bee so he turned back into a snow leopard. This is the gift which nature has given them for their service. Himputra said, "Many here came from distant places. Tomorrow most would return to their habitats, leaving just few behind." Some have come from dark oceans, some from dark pit, some from Antarctica, some from Kalahari Desert. Antarctica is one of the favourite places for yetis as there are no human on that continent. They live along with the penguins and seals. I have visited the snowy continent; it is a paradise for a yeti. Everyone would return to their homeland. These peaks are not homeland for all yetis. This is a myth that yetis are found only in snowy peaks. They could be found in any part of the globe but it should be away from the human eyes. Bidyasagar asked how you travel, suppose you have to go Antartica, how would you go. Himputra said, "We would become birds and would fly and sometime we would turn into fishes when we are near the ocean."

Bidyasagar began reciting a poem dedicated to homeland to celebrate his life in the mountain.

A place where each of us finally want to return,

It is the last place to be like an urn.

We are all tired bee,

Who are tired to see

The pale paintings of barren life.

Every hand holds a knife

Who wants to cut down the glaciers of sorrow

Return to your nest, turn into a sparrow.

The place which makes you happy,

And place where the river of desires meet the sad sea,

Is truly a place to be.

Make your nest in that tree

Whose birds make you feel free.

Bidyasagar was excited to live the life of a yeti. In the morning when he woke up, he found most yetis had left. Himputra asked Bidyasagar to join him for a walk. The sun was rising slowly. The day looked beautiful. Himputra said, "Welcome, Bidyasagar, to the secret clan of yetis. Life is peaceful in the lap of nature."

Himputra continued with more prophesies which now Bidyasagar could also see with his own eyes. How humans would destroy the planet. Greed was Venus fly trap plant which would attract humans like flies. Himputra said, "The snow would disappear from these peaks one day. The forests would go barren. Water which is in plenty and freely available would turn into the most precious item in daily life. Rivers would go dry. The wetlands would turn into barren heaps of dust. Man would imitate nature to the fullest but it would lack the *naturalness*. The cruelty would expand its evil roots to the all territories of life.

There would be artificial photosynthesis, artificial breeding, cloning and finally they will built the artificial man. Life would lose its meaning. The farther they would go from nature the wider the depression would become. The creation of artificial man by man is an event in making.

"There has been negative growth in the mental state of the people with the advent of modern man. The rate of destruction is far beyond the reconstruction of nature. This is a simple logic: if this unbalanced state would continue, nature would disappear."

Bidyasagar saw the future: sea with only domestic fishes, mountains with artificial snow, artificial islands and worst of all: no wildlife. This is the future. There would be climate change. The temperature of the earth would increase to a level that man would not be able to walk out in summer. Thousands of lakes would shrink and get disappear. Everything in nature would get unbalanced, be it climate or ecosystems. The only natural thing would be death. One day man would find remedy to death by finding artificial life which would defy death but at that point, life would be completely meaningless.

Humans would be so bored with the artificial world that one day he would blast the artificial land to sow the seeds of nature. At last man would realize creating artificial man was a mistake but evident for the future growth. This would happen too late, by that time the world will be a mere shadow of future. Humans would crave for nature like he craves to end death. He would crave to end life; he would be disillusioned by his artificial self. He would turn himself into an illusioned being surrounded by an artificial sea.

In the end he would realize nature is irreplaceable but that realization would come too late.

Bidyasagar asked Himputra why men want to recreate nature.

"Man is fond of creating artificial life. Everything has to end; even this human race would end. Humans would create their own end. The end would be tragic like life. The artificial man created by humans would conquer the earth replacing the human race. The artificial man would be ruling the artificial world. Humans are actually creating the ground needed for the artificial man. They would become a victim to a disease they invented out of their own curiosity.

Yetis can live in the archaic nature which man is not capable of. The superficiality would grow to a level that humans would go restless, and insanity will grip them. Nature will be the only relief to humans, not the dosages of the tablets which he would invent to make himself happy. Humans would master the art of imitation. The planet would begin to dry and species after species would disappear from the earth. Humans would be responsible for this extinction. The karma is always acting on the human world.

Humans have been harsh towards Mother Nature and fellow brother species. The elephants, the deer, the wild buffaloes, the jaguars—we are destroying their home but we have forgotten nature is our real home. We are destroying our own home under the illusion of having an artificial home."

Bidyasagar really liked the conversation. Humans had to be stopped at some point otherwise they would destroy the planet which they inherited from other species. But he also knew it very well humans are unstoppable. They would keep rising like a phoenix. Humans turned out to be nature at its best. Their mind works like the devil. They are so clever that it is almost impossible to beat them in any game. Bidyasagar is aware of the potential of humans but they must be stopped.

He knew a war is coming, between the yetis and humans over the discourse of nature. Himputra said, "Yetis will fight for nature until their last breath. They have been hiding from human eyes for centuries because humans would try to domesticate them as well, if they knew of their existence. Soon time would come for yetis to confront the humans. We can no longer remain hidden from humans but they should be given a chance. We want to wait and see the human trajectory of growth in future. Maybe they would find a way to change."

After all Siddhartha was human too. He knew every life deserves compassion. The birth of such people makes us think twice about our actions. They would find a way. Bidyasagar said, "I know man because I have been one, they would not stop. They would go on till they have conquered all the galaxies of the universe. They would not stop until they have known the recipe to create another universe for themselves. They would keep looking for that secret recipe in the chambers of gods. They would make an enemy of gods when they are as powerful as their deities."

Himputra said, "Yetis have decided to wait for a few hundred years to see if man could change his discourse of destruction. We would have enough time to see if man could turn himself to a better species. Himputra further said we would be living till then as we have lived without interfering in the human discourse. Bidyasagar asked what we would do for so long. Himputra answered we would wait and enjoy nature; in this time you would know what it means to be a yeti."

Bidyasagar knows deep in his heart that the war between the yetis and the humans is inevitable. It will take place in future. Yetis believe somewhere humans can change but Bidyasagar knows they will not. That's the beauty; the future we are looking at is completely on the basis of present, if present would change, the future would change with it. The future would change if humans will change.

12

The War

Bidyasagar waited for centuries. The human world was completely transformed, and fast. Humans used their brain as much as they could. Soon industrialization came in. There was change in the way man thought. Industrialization changed everything. There were factories and mills covering the face of the earth. Humans grew more and more ambitious. They began to experiment on everything they could get their hands on. In the modern times, humans used their passion for the destruction of the earth. The earth was in great pain and sorrow. There was no change in their trajectory; the path of destruction was unchanged. There was a massive increase in the scale of destruction. Humans were the central force who had got out of control but wanted to control everything. This was the wild side of humans in the name of good civilization. Bidyasagar prayed at nights for humans but his prayers remained unanswered. They continued to create havoc in the heart of nature, the scale shot up like never before. There were hot scorching summers afternoons like never before. The snow had begun to turn into vapour. The mountains were losing its snow. There was an evil empire of plastic choking the gills of millions of fishes. Species after species began to die out. Earth is almost 4.6 billion old. It took millions of years for earth to start life on its surface and man was ending the same with a strange madness. The prophesies were turning to be true. He was under the spell of an evil shadow named greed. Greed could end everything, and it was doing that at present. The demons in hell were rejoicing at humans' actions. They have walked closer to hell; they have distanced themselves from gods.

Humans had chemicalized the land and sea. It was seeping through the cracked belly of mother earth. The underground water was being mixed with evil soup turning into a poison that killed slowly. Man continued to give more importance to his artificial world against the nature. Bidyasagar could see sadness is growing among humans like shoots of bamboo.

He turned into a lizard and lived for years in the house of Mr Dey as a yeti spy. Mr Dey lived alone in a big luxurious house, his wife was dead and his children lived in other cities. At nights he would wake up, open his gate and go for a walk into the fields. He loved the midnight walk. Bidyasagar saw how lonely Mr Dey was. He had every luxury item he needed, he had machines of all sort doing all the household chores. He cried sometimes in silence; nobody knew a man could cry at nights out of loneliness. He had neighbours but they were too trapped in the snares of modern life. The age of artificial man has begun. Human's life was threatened by the human factors such as deforestation, the falling ground water table and climate change.

Nature was disappearing from the background. There was an evil dream spreading its barren territory in the human life. The human consciousness was filled with the chaos. Everything was being done in the name of great civilization. He observed Mr Dey's life very closely. He ate genetically engineered vegetables which had almost no taste at all. It provided them the nutrients but it lacked taste. There was a similar tastelessness in all spheres of life. He had every possible luxury but he craved for nature. He walked miles to reach the last river of his land. He did it at midnight. He went there in the river with chapattis but the river had lost wild and native fishes, there were alien creatures in the polluted water which feasted upon nothing but garbage. Everything is domesticated according to the human will. Everything is controlled; man was losing its place in the civilization of artificial man. Something was turning him insane. He recognized that unknown element before his death. It was the loss of the depth in the human heart. The water in the heart's sea had become shallow, unsuitable for living. It was the reminiscent of the lost nature which gave little comfort to his aching soul. There was only one thing he was unable to build artificially which was his soul. They could not make souls in their factories. They wanted to get rid of their soul because it craved for nature and there was no nature. They took pills to kill the growing depression. They made them artificially happy but it did not support a long time. They soon began feeling a terrible sadness has engulfed their world. The python of sadness was growing in size; it had devoured the deer of hope. The disillusionment was puzzling. Man had everything but he was not able to figure out why he was sad.

The poor got hit the worst. The last river was walled from all sides and only rich men had access to it. Similarly, the poor were eliminated from the gift of nature. They were made to live in slums. A kilo of organic fruit cost much beyond their monthly income. The organic was reserved for rich man but it was the same world where nature produced everything organically. There was a time, Bidyasagar remembered, when nature was accessible to all. Nature never discriminated but man did.

Bidyasagar could not wait any longer. He came to the mountains and called a meeting of the yetis. He said, "Man has poisoned everything, nature has to be saved. We are already late. We have to do something."

Himputra said, "Karma would take its course. We should let it decide the fate."

"It is already too late. We should've attacked many centuries back. We have given humans enough time to change."

Himputra said, "We won't be able to defeat them. They are beyond defeat now; once they could have been defeated but they are invincible now."

"I know chances are dim but this war is not for victory. We have to get their attention regarding dying state of earth. We have remained hidden for centuries but it's time to leave the invisible cloak and protect the remaining nature."

The yetis began screaming and hooting we would fight. They immediately got to work, defending nature. The news spread in the world of men of attack of yetis. Every yeti turned into their true form. They were walking on their two foot. They were protecting what should have been protected. Many yetis turned into dinosaurs, whales and vultures. Some turned into ancient birds called Pletasauras who could defend Mother Nature. Yetis destroyed their ships, their ports. Man attacked with all their might. They attacked with submarines and airplanes. There was a war between blue whales and submarines in the sea. There were hundreds of yetis who had turned into blue whales and other ancient sea creatures. The yetis turned into everything they could but man had built an artificial self which was powerful than natural self. Nature wanted man to lose but man is not born to lose. There was widespread panic for a while. Humans were not able to believe the creature they thought never existed were actually here. It took them time to figure out these are yetis. Humans were fascinated by their capability to change into any beast they wanted.

The war was quite massive. For days it went on. Yetis had exposed themselves to the human eyes. It was everywhere on the news. After a month the yetis began to lose the grip. Man was winning the battle. Man proved he could kill any beast nature has ever produced. Nature was crying for its soldiers. Yetis were the true patriot of Mother Nature. Man was laughing. They have found one more beast to experiment on.

Man won; yetis were taken prisoners and used by humans to study their genes. Bidyasagar was also caught and sent to a laboratory for experiments. Man was curious to know the secret of Yetis' genes. Now they wanted to build an artificial yeti. Bidyasagar couldn't stop his tears. He wished to be killed but unfortunately survived the war. It was the worst thing that could have happened to him. Those people in the laboratory would never know he was a human once. A man was torturing his own kind under the illusion that he was a different being.

All the yetis were not caught, many had escaped to their hideout. They could be anywhere in any form. They could be a butterfly flying next to our cities. Himputra left the high mountains and turned into a fish. He swam and reached the bottom of the ocean. He knew man would be searching for the yetis now. It was only in the ocean and deep forests where they were safe.

The man was looking for ways to locate the yetis. They were searched everywhere but it was impossible to find them in the ocean of animal forms. They have known the yetis' deep secret that they could take form of any creature lived in the past or present. They could turn into gigantic dinosaurs but man was capable of defeating any creature of past and present. He was the king of all beasts but never claims to be a beast. Humans rather pretend to be civilized but the reality is far from it.

Bidyasagar was tortured night and day with all sorts of experiments. The samples of yeti cells were being collected for further experimentation. Bidyasagar began feeling his end would come soon. There was rare chance that he could escape men's hell in any way. He began counting his days. Himputra was out in the beds of ocean. He knew man could not catch him if he lived in the company of sea creatures.

There were only a few hundred Yetis left in the wilderness. They took refuge in the remotest place they could find.

A lot changed after the invention of the Yeti machine. Many more yetis were recognized and caught by the machines. Many men turned into yeti hunters. They became the most prized beast of all. The yetis which ran were in danger again if they turned into true yeti form. It appeared yeti had no choice but to turn into something which is very dear to men.

Himputra too realized they could not escape the human shadow. The freedom of the yetis was in the hand of men. Freedom is the most basic need of life for any creature. Man wants freedom for himself but not for the yetis. Everyday few yetis were caught since the advent of yeti machine but not all yetis could be caught. Many yetis began to live in other forms of life. Himputra soon realized yetis have to fight for their freedom, if not they would be turned into a domesticated slave whom man would use for their amusement. He remembered the words of Bidyasagar, fight for nature until death. Himputra decided to unite the remaining yetis for another war against the humans. It was better to die free than dying as a piece of human experiment. They did not want humans to interfere with their genes as they had done to numerous creatures. There is nothing like freedom.

All the yetis united under the leadership of Himputra. They knew they would get killed. They wanted to die rather than live in cages. Cages are the last thing anybody wants for themselves. Himputra said to the united members of yeti community, "We have to die, die as ferocious lions. We are the soldiers of nature. We have to fight against humans knowing we would be doomed forever after the war. There might be just few of us left after the war. Those who will live should remember what it is to be a yeti. They should preserve the yetiness in them."

Man soon realized another yeti war is coming. The yetis fought the empire of men. Every yeti turned into a T-rex and charged at them. It was tough to tackle hundreds of T-rexes all at once. Man had a tough time. Cities after cites were destroyed. It was the rage of nature. It was not the yetis fighting; it was the nature fighting for its survival. Man used their best of machines to fight the yeti. Yetis were losing lives, fighting artificial machines. Very few men died but yetis died in large numbers.

Man won even this war. Yetis were turned into another fancy species which man used for his amusement. Bidyasagar began thinking his last poem

The Last Letter to Humans

A species blended with blood and iron,

Who wants to turn every heron

Into a hen, even to that wild wren.

There has to be a law guiding the hell and heaven.

Man oh man be kind, soon it would be your turn.

I know you have been champions but learn

To respect the other forms of life.

Throw away the greedy knife

And once walk through the woods with an open mind.

You will see it's not hard to be kind.

I am dying here in a glass cell.

Learn from the mighty whale,

Have a big heart,

Because it hurts

When we are turned into an amusement.

We want to be wild and free,

Every insect cannot be your domesticated bee.

I have been human and known your taste for blood

And even had walked through the human mud.

Still you want your feet to be clean.

Trees once were growing thick like hell, now they grow
thin.

The world will burn up in flames of your evil laughter.

Break the dams and let the rivers

Flow through the wild landscape.

I know there is no kingdom of beasts in your secret map.

Remember laws of nature are one and same

For fire and flame.

Don't save us but yourselves from greed.

Don't be a cruel breed,

Cruelty will take you nowhere.

I know you love to stare the starry hare

Running in the black space.

Saving us will only save the human race.

We are all connected,

That's why we all will be affected.

If the nature goes

Then this beautiful world will no longer remain a rose.

The earth will become a desert.

Men oh men have a big heart.

You have forgotten what it takes to be human.

The deadly sins are not seven,

There is one more, cruelty.

Man oh man, understand every insect could not be a domesticated bee.

Every bird cannot be a hen.

There has to be eagle, hawks and wren

Flying high in the sky.

I know you have learnt to fly

But don't make a fool of you.

Leave the old path, create a new.

Siddhartha was one, Gandhi another.

Remember we are all brothers

And son of same god.

Time has come, choose a wise road.

Bidyasagar died with the poem in his head. He wanted to speak the words out loud but he was locked inside a glass chamber. He peeped into his past; he could remember everything from life of a hunter to a respected master of Nalanda and his life as a yeti. He could see clearly now, how human race would end by the artificial man, in the same way as nature was ended by humans. Outside, people were walking through the streets, unaware the nature was crying but it knew his son had abandoned her forever. Man is no more human but a collection of ultra-modern strain who knows nothing but to kill nature at every step. They tried to save Mother Nature but his son was too thirsty of blood of nature. The last thing Bidyasagar realized before his death, human growth is inevitable and it would take place. The growth is not the problem but the negative growth is. Man would understand one day protecting nature is imminent for him. Many yetis would have died but their spirit would always be with nature. Man too would begin to protect nature. They would understand why yetis fought the war. They would realize the mistake of growing without nature is a costly affair. Nature must be saved for our survival. The soul of Bidyasagar would keep wandering in space waiting for man to change his attitude towards nature. This tale would always remain in the human consciousness, a species fought for nature and we were against it. We were too busy establishing the natureless artificial empire.

The very few Yetis who survived the war ran off to distant places including Himputra. He went into the high mountains and turned back into a snow leopard. He would cry for the death of his friends, alone in the wilderness.